Christmas in
Reverence Ridge
Elaina Kellogg

To my Fuzzball and Big Man, who keep life entertaining and full.
Love you forever and ever.

And to all who keep the kindness and generosity of the holiday spirit
alive and well. Sprinkle that stuff everywhere!

Contents

Optional Playlist

Since carols and music are such a big part of holiday celebrations, I selected a song to accompany each story. Hopefully it will add another layer to your reading experience. Singing along is encouraged.

Chris: White Christmas by Bing Crosby

Caroline: Silver Bells by Martina McBride

Taylor: Have Yourself a Merry Little Christmas by Frank Sinatra

Macy: We Need a Little Christmas by Pentatonix

Everleigh: Run Rudolph Run by Chuck Berry

Warrick: Christmas Tree Farm by Taylor Swift

Viola: Where are you Christmas by Faith Hill

Celia: All I Want for Christmas Is You by Mariah Carey

Nora: It's Beginning to Look a Lot Like Christmas by Johnny Mathis

Chris

THURSDAY, DECEMBER 16

"One Dasher doughnut and a Happy Holey-Glaze, please."

Chris watched the woman behind the counter pull out a thick chocolate doughnut, dripping ganache, and slid it onto a pristine plate. That was followed by a fat, glossy one dotted with snowflake sprinkles. He eyed the rest of the pastry case, filled with all kinds of breakfast delights. Cinnamon rolls that oozed frosting. Scones coated in glistening sugar crystals. Spice muffins dusted with powdered sugar.

"Come on, dear. You don't need any extras." Birdie patted his belly with a grin. "Besides, we need to hurry. We've got a busy day."

Chris rubbed his stomach and had to agree. The buttons on his worn, flannel shirt struggled to hold it closed. Birdie slid her hand into his elbow as they slowly made their way to their usual table in the front window. Chris pulled out a chair for his wife before sitting across from her. They easily fell into a rhythm of placing out napkins, dividing out the food, and setting out their coffee mugs from home. Chris's big, clunky one reading "This is my Bah Hum Mug" dwarfed his wife's delicate mug covered in poinsettias.

Kind of like us. Chris smiled at the thought.

"What are you grinning at?" Birdie asked. "Do I have powdered sugar on me or something?"

"No. No." Chris shook his head and picked up his doughnut. "You look as beautiful as the day I met you."

"Oh, you old ham." Birdie swatted at him playfully, but Chris could see the slight blush in her cheeks as she ducked her head. The edges of her eyes crinkled with her smile. She hated the wrinkles that had developed there, but Chris said they were evidence of a happy life.

"It's nice to know I can still make you blush after all these years," Chris said softly and laid his hand on the table, palm up.

Birdie scooched her chair closer and slid her hand into his. They both turned to watch as the sun slowly rose outside the picture window over Reverence Ridge, their peaceful, little town. The fog lifted off the city square, revealing the surrounding shops built of warm wooden beams, the town hall and courthouse at the center, and the white plank church at the far end. Tall pines filled the sky above the buildings, the tips still shrouded in mist. Chris and Birdie's hands remained entwined on the table, and by the time they finished their pastries, the sun shone weakly through low, gray clouds.

"Looks like snow today," the coffee shop owner, Mindy, said as she came over with a pitcher of coffee in each hand.

"Hopefully just a dusting." Birdie pulled her hand out of Chris's and tucked it in her lap. "We don't want anything messing with the parade tomorrow."

"Is that tomorrow already?" Chris's thick eyebrows pulled together.

"Oh, you jokester. Like anyone in this town could forget the parade. Decaf." Mindy poured coffee into Birdie's mug and then switched hands to pour into Chris's. "Caf. Give you a little extra boost to get through today, huh?"

"Humph." Chris grunted.

"We definitely have a lot going on." Birdie patted his hand on the table. "All of us do."

"But more for Mr. C than most." Mindy nudged his shoulder with her elbow.

Chris didn't say anything, just raised his mug in salute and took a long drink, allowing the warmth to flow through him. He closed his eyes and took a deep breath as Birdie and Mindy talked about all the plans for the next few weeks, and there were many. This was the busiest time of year for him with Christmas around the corner. Tomorrow would be the kick-off parade for the holiday season. Their humble little town went all out and drew more tourists over the next couple weeks than the rest of the year combined. He ran his fingers through his long beard, thinking about all the work ahead.

Bells chimed as more customers entered the coffee shop. Mindy returned to the counter while Chris and Birdie sat a while longer. Soon, the shop was filled with happy chatter and laughter. Outside, snowflakes began floating to the ground leaving just a hint of the mountains in the distance.

"I suppose it's time to get moving, don't you think?" Birdie asked as she wiped their mugs with a napkin and slid them back into her bag. "We need to find presents for the grandkids and stop by the Tin Soldier for groceries. I was thinking we'd do turkey instead of ham this year since we're watching your sodium. And Lord knows how much sodium is in ham."

Chris nodded while he gathered their trash. He helped slide her chair out as she stood, and they wound their way towards the door. Chris stopped to help Birdie into her coat as she chatted with the Wilson's from church. They waved their farewells and walked out into the fresh morning air.

"I think we should save the groceries for last." Birdie pulled her collar up around her chin. "How about we head to Wizzle's first for the grandkids?"

They turned left and started down the sidewalk, but Chris stopped and grabbed onto Birdie's arm. He stared at her for a moment. Soft snowflakes fell, disappearing into her white hair. He placed a hand on her cheek, both more aged and wrinkled than when they first met all those years ago. Their looks had changed considerably since their younger years, but her bright eyes had never lost their sparkle.

He slid his hand down around her shoulder and turned them both to look out over the town square. Even in the chill, people were flitting about like hummingbirds in a flower garden. Men from Callaway Construction strung lights in the trees. They'd just finished hanging fresh pine garland on the gazebo in the center of the square. All the store fronts had been filled with an assortment of nutcrackers, reindeer, and elves. Speakers atop flickering lamp posts filled the air with We Wish You a Merry Christmas. Snow fell quietly, making everything feel softer, gentler.

"This really is the most wonderful time of the year," Chris murmured. "I want to soak this all in. Memorize it so I never forget how beautiful it is."

"Hmmm." Birdie snuggled into his embrace. "Pretty sure after over sixty years here, this place is burned into our brains. We couldn't forget it if we wanted to."

They stood a moment longer, quiet amongst the bustle. Chris's mind wandered and landed on a thread he'd been pulling at for sometime. A constant nagging ache he'd been afraid to dissect or share. His heart suddenly felt like thundering reindeer hooves in his chest. The scene in front of him lost the serene feeling of moments before, becoming chaotic and overwhelming instead.

"I don't think I can do it this year," Chris blurted.

"Do what?" Birdie lifted her head up to look at him, her brows creased in concern.

"I can't..." Chris looked around them and lowered his voice, "be Santa. I can't do it anymore."

"Oh pish." Birdie flicked a hand at him. "Your knees will be fine. Just don't let the big kids sit on you as long this year."

"It's not that." He rubbed his forehead. "I just...I've been thinking about it a lot. I can't do it."

"You're serious?" Birdie turned to face him, splaying both hands on his jacket, her eyes searching his. "You're really serious?"

Chris lowered his eyes, not wanting to meet the concern in hers, and nodded. Her hands slid down his jacket to her sides. His stomach churned waiting for all the questions, the pity, the disappointment.

"Well," Birdie squawked, "in all my years."

Chris's head snapped up, surprised at the anger in her voice. She started pacing in front of him, four quick steps one way, four back the other way. He squared his shoulders, ready when she finally turned his way again.

"Christopher Countryman. You have been the Santa for this town for over thirty years. And now, the day before the big parade, you're telling me you can't do it anymore? And you've been thinking about it a lot? Why haven't I heard of this? We're a team, aren't we?"

"Of course." The corner of Chris's mouth raised slightly. He always loved it when she got feisty. It was one of her finest qualities.

"Don't you smirk at me, mister." She poked a trembling finger into his chest. "Why in the blazes didn't you mention this before?"

"I wasn't sure."

"You weren't sure?" She threw her hands up and started pacing again, her voice raising even louder. "He wasn't sure. But today, today of all days he decides to be sure. Why not just wait until tomorrow, then we can really leave the town in a lurch with no Santa for the Christmas season?"

Chris looked past Birdie and realized all the folks around the square had stopped hanging lights. Stopped decorating. Stopped their shopping. Everyone had stopped to listen.

"Birdie, darling, maybe we should talk about this somewhere else." He placed a hand on her elbow to stop her pacing.

"Don't you 'darling' me. You chose to bring it up here, so here we shall talk."

"Maybe we should go somewhere a little more...private." He raised his eyebrows and gestured around them.

That got her attention, and she looked around for the first time. Seeing all the eyes on them cooled her anger for the moment. She cleared her throat and patted at her hair, still neatly in a bun at the back of her neck.

"Maybe you're right." She pulled her purse strap tighter onto her shoulder and slid her hand into his elbow. "We can discuss this more at home."

"There's nothing to discuss, dear." He curled his fingers through hers as they made their way down the sidewalk. "My mind's made up."

"We'll see about that."

Birdie raised her chin but refused to look at him as they walked into Wizzle's Wonders. Warm air, heavy with the scent of apple cider and cinnamon, greeted them when they walked into the shop. Glossy wooden shelves covered with toys of all shapes and sizes filled the small space. Airplanes whizzed in circles overhead. Trains puffed down tracks along the walls. Several families crowded the tight aisles.

"Why don't you look at something for Jax while I go look for Amelia?"

Birdie still didn't look at him but took off down an aisle towards the back of the store. Chris watched her until she was out of sight. He tugged at the collar of his jacket, which suddenly felt too snug. This store normally filled him with a wonder, but today it felt too claustrophobic. His eyes darted from one thing to the next, unsure where to settle.

A little boy bounded down the aisle and stopped in front of him. The boy beamed up at Chris with a huge grin.

"You're him, aren't you?" His words whistled through the gap where his two front teeth should have been. "You're Santa."

"Um. Oh" Chris glanced up, hoping to see Birdie, but she was out of sight. "Hello there."

"You look just like all the pictures. Even the long beard." He put his hands on his hips and scowled. "It isn't fake, is it?"

"Well, I could tell you that it's real, but you probably wouldn't believe me, would you?" When the boy shook his head, Chris kneeled and smiled. "Why don't you give it a tug and find out for yourself."

The boy reached out and give his beard a quick yank. He gasped with delight when it stuck fast, making Chris chuckle.

"Believe me now? Good. So, what do you want for Christmas this year?"

The little boy stepped forward and whispered in his ear all the things he wished for. Chris was nodding and listening when a young man rounded the corner and stopped next to them.

"Oh, there you are. I'm so sorry, sir," he said as he placed a hand on the boy's shoulder.

"It's ok, Daddy" the boy said. "I was just telling Santa what I wanted for Christmas."

"Oh, were you?" His dad smiled down at him. "Why don't you go find mom?"

"Ok." He looked up at Chris, hope radiating from his face. "Don't forget, Santa!"

"I'll try not to," Chris muttered, but the boy had already run off down the aisle.

"Um. I'm not sure if this falls under Santa etiquette or not, but could you give me a hint at what he wants? He wouldn't even let us read the letter he wrote to Santa, erm, you, this year."

"I think Santa etiquette dictates that all kids should get what they want for Christmas." Chris stood up, his knees cracking in protest, and lowered his voice. "He wants a firetruck. With lights, siren, and batteries."

"Ahhhh. That makes sense. My brother just became a fireman." The dad patted Chris on the back. "Thanks, um, Santa."

"Merry Christmas."

Chris's feeling of fulfillment quickly faded as he glanced around, not sure what he was supposed to do next. The air felt too sweet and warm. He turned in a quick circle looking for Birdie but didn't see her. Something pulled at his memory, something he was supposed to be doing.

"Excuse me." A woman with arms full of toys squeezed past.

Chris pressed himself against the shelves. He was just in the way here. He frowned as he tried to think of why he was at Wizzle's in the first place, but when his mind came up blank, he decided it best to get out of the cramped aisles.

The cold, outside air helped to clear some of the fog in his mind as he went to stand on the curb. Thick, heavy snowflakes were tumbling from the clouds now. He could almost hear the plopping of each one as the roads and sidewalks turned to slush. He was staring intently at the tire tracks in the road when the door opened behind him.

"There you are. Chris? Earth to Chris."

He snapped his head up, pulling his mind from the swirl around them. He opened his arms and pulled Birdie into a warm embrace.

"Brrr. It's getting cold fast." She shivered in his arms. "What in the world are you doing out here?"

"I think I just got overheated."

"Did you find a good gift for Jax? I still say gift giving is your superpower, not mine."

"Oh, that boy in the store? I don't remember." Chris run a hand through his long beard. "I think he told me what he wanted..."

"That boy in the store? Chris, I'm talking about Jax...our grandson."

"Oh, of course. Was I supposed to be finding a gift?"

"Of course. Why else would we be here?" Birdie puled him close and stood on her tiptoes to get her face as close to his as possible. She grasped his chin and turned his face from side to side. "Are you feeling ok?"

"Like I said, just a little overheated." He smiled at her and kissed the tip of her nose. "I'm fine now. Let's go get Jax's gift. I think I have an idea now."

They went back into the shop and several minutes later walked back out with several large bags. The snow had stopped, leaving behind a layer of wet snow. The kind that would be melted within the hour but then freeze overnight.

"Gonna be slick tomorrow," he muttered as they picked their way around puddles.

"You're probably right. I hope the parade is ok."

"It doesn't start until 10. Should be fine by then."

"And your float isn't until the very end, so everything should be nice and thawed."

"Birdie..."Chris sighed.

"It's a little late to back out now."

They reached their car parked across from the coffeeshop, Cup of Cheer, and loaded the bags into the trunk. Chris was thinking about running in for another doughnut when Birdie disappeared around the side of the car with a squeal of delight.

Their friends, Roxie and Stew, had just walked out pushing a stroller. Birdie was peeking under the blanket that covered their little granddaughter.

"Oh, Roxie. She's just so precious." Birdie cooed. "Hi sweet girl."

Chris reached out to shake with Stew, then stuffed his hands into his pockets. Birdie held up the blanket and he peeked inside.

"Hey there, cutie. Is that a smile? I see that smile." He couldn't help but smile back.

"It always amazes me how fast they grow." Birdie said. "It's only been a week since we saw you and she already seems so much bigger."

"Right?" Roxie said. "Pretty soon she'll be off to college."

"And then grown and having babies of her own." Birdie clutched at her heart and swooned.

"Well, let's not plan her whole life away." Stew shook his head and laughed. "Maybe she should learn to sit up or talk first?"

"You know it's fun to imagine." Roxie chuckled. "There's so many possibilities."

"She could be top of her class." Birdie suggested.

"Or be the best goalie our soccer team has ever seen." Chris offered.

"Maybe she'll become an international rock sensation and change her name to a symbol no one can pronounce." Roxie smiled down at the stroller. "We just never know.

"Oh, names! That reminds me." Birdie turned to Chris and said, "What was that nickname you came up with for her the other day?"

"Um." Chris stopped smiling, trying to remember, but nothing came to mind. "I came up with a nickname?"

"Yes, you did. We were laughing about it all evening." Birdie tapped his arm with the back of her hand. "Oh, come on, don't you remember? It rhymes with her name."

"Her name." Chris muttered and frowned. "Um...I..."

Chris looked down at the baby, so bundled up all you could see were her chubby cheeks and dark brown eyes. He'd rocked her to sleep countless times after church. Their families got together for dinner almost every week. And as he stood there, staring at her smiling face, his chest tightened and his mind was a blank.

"Oh, I remember." Birdie fluttered a hand at him. "He said we should call her Mia instead of Amelia, so she wouldn't be confused with our little Amelia. And if she went by Mia, she'd just have to be Mia Tortilla."

Around him, everyone laughed, but the sound didn't quite reach his ears. All he heard was the blood pounding in his head. A feeling of dread, that he was becoming much too familiar with, flooded his system. His stomach simultaneously feltlike it dropped down into his shoes and tied up in a knot making it hard to breathe.

"Chris. Chris?"

Stew's voice broke through to him. Chris looked up from the stroller, his eyes still wide and his breathing shallow.

"What's this I hear about you not being Santa?" Stew clapped him on the back. "Mayor Davenport didn't say anything about needing a new Santa. Or maybe I'd have tried out for the part."

"Well, there goes the gossip mill again." Birdie shook her head. "She didn't say anything because Chris hasn't...isn't turning in his hat just yet."

"Phew." Roxie wiped her brow. "That's a relief. You're always the highlight of the season for the kids around here."

"Yep." Stew nodded. "No one can 'Ho. Ho. Ho.' quite like you."

"Thanks guys." Chris cleared his tight throat. "But, I haven't decided yet. I think it might just be time to pass on the reins."

"Well, you better make up your mind before the town meeting tonight," Stew said." After that, I don't think anyone would hold Caroline- I mean, Mayor Davenport, accountable for her actions."

"Well, we better get this little one in the car." Roxie patted Birdie's arm. "We'll see you tonight?"

"Of course." Birdie's voice was icy as she stared daggers at Chris.

They climbed into their car in silence and parked in silence. Chris mutely pushed the cart through Tin Soldier General as Birdie got all the trimmings for a delicious, albeit low sodium, holiday dinner. Over the next week, as the town filled with tourists, the pickings would get pretty slim. All the locals knew to get the essentials early before they ran out. After a few aisles, Birdie's shoulders lost some of their rigidity, and she began to hum along with the tunes playing over the speakers. Chris took the break from talking as a chance to gather his thoughts.

He wasn't quite ready to put them into words, to make them real, but at least he could organize them in his mind.

Not that it will make any difference.

Chris pushed the cart through the sludgy snow out to the car and loaded the trunk while Birdie waited inside and chatted with a few friends. When he returned the cart, he waited for her to finish and then walked her out, arm in arm.

Birdie didn't talk on the way home. Chris looked over at her several times, but she just stared out the window. The paved road disappeared as they turned into their gravel drive. The pine branches hung low with the heavy snow. Aside from the squelching of their tires, it was completely quiet. Usually, he relished the calm of their little mountain retreat, but today it felt lonely, oppressive.

He pulled into the garage and helped carry in the groceries. Birdie still hadn't said a word. He watched her a moment as she bent to put coffee into the cabinet and pressed her hand into her back as she stood up. He sighed deeply, knowing what needed to happen.

"I know I've disappointed you, my love." He walked over and when he clasped her hand, there was a slight tremor in his. "But I think it's time to talk."

Birdie gave a slight nod and turned back to the counter. Chris slid into a seat at their table while she made two cups of tea. Hers with milk. His plain. He ran his hands over the tabletop. He'd chopped down the tree and built it himself when he was young. He glanced up at the curtains that Birdie had sewn before the kids were born. Then over at the pictures on the wall. All their smiling faces through the years. So many beautiful memories. So many already forgotten.

"Alright. Let's hear it then." Birdie slid into the seat next to his and placed the mugs between them.

Chris looked out the window. It was snowing again. Not the gentle tumble of flakes like this morning. In the dying light, snowflakes swirled through the trees. The wind blew them this way and that, rushing them across the ground before they disappeared into the darkening night.

"That." Chris pointed to the window. "That's what my mind feels like."

Birdie turned to look out the window, and then back at him in confusion.

"I don't understand, honey."

"My thoughts. My memories." Chris squeezed his eyes shut. He swallowed hard, not wanting to say what came next. "It's like they're all there but I just can't find them anymore. Like everything is always just out of reach."

"Ok." Birdie reached across the table and clasped both of his hands in hers. "Explain this to me some more."

"I'm starting to forget, my love." The weight in his chest was crushing.

"Amelia's name today?" Birdie whispered.

Chris nodded.

"And Jax's gift at Wizzle's?"

He nodded again and hung his head, not wanting to see the look on her face.

"And I feel confused. Foggy. A lot." His voice sounded harsh in the silent house.

"Oh, my darling." Birdie pulled his hands closer, wringing them through hers. "Why? Why didn't you tell me?"

"Cause words make it real. This can't be real." He looked up at her them with tears welling in his eyes. "This can't be it."

"This isn't it." Birdie shook her head fiercely. "There's still so much more for us. You have to believe that."

Chris pushed away from the table, unable to sit any longer. Even though he tried to stop them, hot tears leaked from his eyes. Running into his beard. He pulled a hand through the rough hair, wiping away what he could of the wetness.

"It's already getting worse. First it was just little things, like what I came into the room for. Now I'm forgetting people's names. What next, Birdie? Do I start forgetting how to take care of myself? How to take care of the house?" His voice rose with his anger. "Do I start forgetting people all together? Will I forget you? Our kids? The life we've lived together?"

Those final questions hung in the air, frozen. His greatest fears laid bare. He pounded his fist into the wooden mantle unable to contain the emotion building up inside him. Something crashed to the floor behind him, shattering.

Birdie rose from the table and made her way to him. He didn't turn. He wasn't ready to face her. He'd waited so long to avoid the look of pity he knew would be in her eyes.

"Christopher Countryman. Turn around and face me like the man I know you are."

His ears and heart perked up at the tone in her voice. There was no pity there. No disappointment. Just that ferocity he admired so much. He lifted his head and turned to her.

She wrapped him in her arms, holding him tightly before reaching up to hold his face in her hands. Her thumbs brushed away the remainder of the tears on his cheeks.

"We're a team, you and I. Aren't we?"

"Of course." The corner of his mouth rose slightly.

"Then we'll get through this together."

"Why did I ever doubt you, my love?"

"I honestly don't know." She smiled at him then and his heart stuttered.

The weight he'd been carrying so long in his chest lifted and he took the first deep breath he'd taken in a very long time. Placing a hand overtop hers, he closed his eyes and leaned into her touch.

"We promised in sickness and health, and I don't plan to go back on that promise. I've got too many years in this to give up now." She leaned into him. "I won't let you forget. If it gets to that point."

"If anyone could do that, it'd be you, love."

"And this is why you don't want to be Santa anymore?" She pulled back to see his face.

"I love to see the kids' eyes light up when I already know their names. If I can't even remember Amelia, who we see all the time, how am I supposed to remember all the kids from church and the school?" Chris frowned. "Or what if I got foggy and confused when a kid is sitting on my lap. It could ruin their Santa experience for life. I couldn't do that."

"I understand now. I think what you're doing is really admirable." Birdie smiled, tight lipped and bittersweet. "I know how much that job means to you."

"It wasn't just a job." Chris reached up and ruffled his beard. "It was a way of life."

"I know, dear. You really *were* Santa. Whoever Caroline- I mean Mayor Davenport finds to replace you will have big boots to fill."

"Yup." Slowly he let her go and took a step back. "I guess I'd better get the ol' suit packed up to take to the meeting then."

"Do you want help?"

"I think I'd like to do this on my own."

"Ok." Birdie gave his hand a quick squeeze before turning towards the kitchen. "I'll just get some soup on for dinner."

Chris made his way past the Christmas tree, stopping to turn on the flickering white lights and adjust a few ornaments. The wooden boards creaked under his boots as he walked down the hall to the bedroom. He pushed the door open and saw the suit hanging in their open wardrobe. His steps slowed as he took in the dark red jacket with creamy fur cuffs. He pulled out his handkerchief and polished the golden buttons until they shone.

He ran his fingers over some stitching on one elbow where Birdie had patched a small tear from the one and only year they'd rented live reindeer. He couldn't help but smile. He turned the pants around to the back and found the small bald patch in the velvet, the result of cutting out the piece of gum little Jimmy Masterson had left on Santa's chair. Pretty sure that had landed him on the naughty list that year, but he grew out of it and was now the town dentist. He reached down to the black boots and grabbed the polish out of the wardrobe. He gently brushed the polish into the soft leather. Back and forth. For the last time.

"Hey, you doing ok?" Birdie asked from the doorway.

"I'll be glad to not smell this foul stuff again." Chris tried to joke, but Birdie's raised eyebrow told him she wasn't buying it. "Lots of memories here. A whole lot of wonderful memories."

"There sure are." She was silent for a moment. "So, I had a bit of a harebrained idea. Tell me I'm crazy if you want."

"I'm listening."

"Well, if you want to go all in on this new stage in our lives, maybe really let go of the old?" She held up an electric razor with a grin.

Chris ran his fingers through his beard, like he did a hundred times a day. He'd grown it out after his first year as the town Santa. Wearing the fake beard had left him so itchy his face looked like he'd rolled around in poison ivy. Now, would it just be a constant reminder of what he'd given up?

"Let's do it."

"Seriously?" Birdie laughed. "I did *not* think you were going to go for it."

"Well, thanks for the vote of confidence."

"No. No. I think it's a beautifully symbolic gesture. Let's do this."

An hour later, and several pounds lighter, Chris and Birdie parked outside the town hall. The snow was gently falling again, a needed cover for the frozen slush from that morning. As he got out of the car, Chris scrubbed his bare chin.

"What have you done to me, woman?" Chris's teeth chattered. "My cheeks are freezing. How do you stand this?"

"Why do you think ladies have fancy scarves?" Birdie asked as she wrapped hers around her neck and shimmied her shoulders to push it up higher over her cheeks. "I'd be happy to lend you one. Purple would be a lovely color on you."

Chris pulled a garment bag from the back seat and threw it over his arm. His other arm he used to escort his wife to the door. His hand barely touched the knob before it flew open, and they were yanked inside.

"Aunt Birdie. Uncle Chris. Thank God. I thought you'd never get here."

"Hello, dear." Birdie kissed the young woman with dark hair on the cheek and started to shrug off her coat. "I assume it's him you're wanting."

"Hello, Caroline- I mean Mayor Davenport." Chris bent down and kissed her on the other cheek.

"Uncle Chris. Is that even you?" She reached out and poked at one of his newly exposed cheeks, a look like she'd just taken a bite of lemon crossed her face. "I've literally never seen you without your glorious beard."

"I'm turning over a new leaf you might say."

"Please, please, please tell me the rumors aren't true." She clasped her hands in front of her. "Please tell me you aren't retiring."

"I'm afraid I must." Chris held out the garment bag, but she refused to take it, waving her hands in front of her.

"No. No. No. This is my first Christmas on the job, Uncle Chris. You *cannot* do this to me. My career will be over before it's even begun."

"Caroline, you're going to have to trust me. It's time." Chris's shoulders sank. "I wish I could have given you more notice. For that, I'm very sorry."

"I do trust you. I know you wouldn't make this decision lightly." She locked her eyes with his. "But just be honest with me. Are you ok? Job be damned. Family first."

"I'm just getting too old. Besides, no matter what, with Birdie and you by my side, I'll be just fine."

She reached out and took the garment bag from his outstretched arm and then stepped in to give him a hug. After a final squeeze, she let him go.

"Well, I want to be the first to thank you for so many wonderful childhood memories." She dabbed at her eye with the back of a finger. "And I know I'm not the only one."

They walked out of the foyer and into the common room. People stood in small groups around the room, talking in hushed tones. A table weighed down with cookies and treats sat in one corner. One by one, the groups fell silent as they noticed Chris in the room. Slowly, a round of applause spread through them all, starting as a pitter patter and growing into a roar. Chris stopped in his tracks, stunned. Birdie clasped his hand, smiling up at him with tears in her eyes. The clapping continued until Caroline raised her hands for silence.

"As you all guessed, the rumors are true. Our town Santa of many, many years has decided to turn in his hat." Caroline addressed the crowd. She raised a hand over her eyes and began searching the room. "Now, if my Uncle Chris could step up so we can properly thank him... I'm sure he's just off combing and conditioning his beard somewhere. Oh, wait. Who's this?"

The laughter broke through the somber mood and soon everyone was cracking jokes and making jabs about his missing beard. One by one, everyone walked over showing Chris pictures with their children or of themselves when they were young sitting on his lap at Christmas. Most pressed the photos into his hands, telling him how much he meant to their Christmas memories. All Chris could do was listen and nod as the stack of photos in his hands grew.

In his heart, he knew that if he eventually didn't remember every single one of them, this feeling of joy and purpose would stay with him forever. And that even if *he* didn't remember, *they* all would.

After the last person returned to their seat, Chris cleared his throat, but before he could speak, someone hollered from the back of the room.

"Did you have to use a bushwhacker to get all that hair off?"

"It was a symbolic gesture, ok?" Chris threw up his hands then paused for a moment, looking through the photos he held. "I can't even begin to tell you all what this means to me. You all have given me the best gift I could have asked for. Being Santa has been the joy of my life. Whoever is lucky enough to wear that suit next is very, very blessed indeed."

"Speaking of which..." Caroline stepped up next to him, "We're needing to fill those boots very quickly, so if you're interested, see me tonight. Chris was kind enough to turn over his suit, and I believe there's even a fake beard in there. So, no pressure to compete with this guy's facial hair growing abilities until next year."

"Oh, there will be pressure." Chris raised a finger. "These cheeks were not made forthe eyes of mortals or this frigid weather. The beard regrowing starts now."

Caroline

C aroline chugged her peppermint mocha like her life depended on it. And with the way her day started, her life very well may depend on copious amounts of caffeine and sugar. At barely 8 a.m. she'd already downed two cookies, a gingerbread scone, and wasn't about to waste the candy cane she'd been using to stir her mocha.

"I have the finalized line-up for you, Mrs. Mayor."

"Thank you, Presley." Caroline snatched the paper from her assistant's hand and scoured the list. "The Reverence High Band can't go after the park rangers. We can't have our teens marching through horse poop."

"Who would you suggest then, ma'am?" Presley tapped her lip with her pen. "Who is ok to step in poop?"

"No one, Presley!" Caroline snapped, then closed her eyes and reached out to place a hand on Presley's shoulder. "Sorry. Put the nursing home knitters after the rangers. They move slow enough we can hire a couple kids to get in there with pooper scoopers before they step in anything."

"Great idea, ma'am."

"Ok. Get me a final-final line-up and find some kids who will scoop poop for sugar cookies. Throw in a couple hot chocolates if that's too difficult."

"On it. Right away."

Presley hurried from the office, her dark curls and the bells on her bracelet bouncing with each step. The entire mayoral team wore matching bracelets covered with tiny silver bells. Jim from IT complained it made him feel like a cat, but Caroline thought they added to the festivity of the day and would make it easier to find each other when they were rushing between floats and parade participants. They also all wore gray shirts with a little shimmer to them. Not so much as to call them silver, but enough that it made the guys in the office grumble. Adding the words "Sleigh, what?" in massive print was the cherry on top as far as Caroline was concerned.

Moments later, a fresh line-up was printed and on her desk. Jim's two boys were chugging hot chocolate in the corner and fencing with pooper scoopers. Caroline looked with pride around the office at the nine others who made up her team. She'd picked each member with care, and they were officially the youngest and most diverse mayoral team that Reverence Ridge had ever had.

"All right team." She raised her hand and jiggled the bracelet, creating a lovely tinkling high pitched enough to be heard above the typical office noise. "I don't have to tell y'all how important today is. I also don't have to tell you how much I appreciate each and every one of you, but I'm going to anyway. Y'all are miracle workers. You're my life force, and I cannot thank you enough for all the work you've put in to make today possible."

Everyone hooted and cheered. Then they all raised their bracelets in the air and jingled them at her with a laugh. Caroline beamed at her team.

"Now, let's give this town the best Christmas parade they've ever seen." Caroline pumped her fists in the air. Then she raised a finger and said, "Remember- Spread some cheer, but stay near so you can hear."

She raised her bracelet and jingled it again. This time everyone groaned. She'd drilled that motto into their heads over the past few weeks. The previous mayor said one of the biggest issues with last year's parade was communication between staff. So, without having to commit to the squeaks and squawks you get with walkie talkies, this was her solution.

"You're gonna wear that arm out before we leave the office," someone hollered.

"Yeah. Yeah. Just stay close and be ready for the unexpected."

"What about Santa?" Jim asked.

"I'm on it, Jim." She patted her clipboard. "I had several gentlemen express interest at the town hall last night and they will be meeting me this morning for a final decision. No fear, our parade WILL end with the jolly man himself. Now, Roll out!"

As everyone headed for the door, Caroline stopped Jim's boys for a pep talk and basic pooper scooper instruction.

"Boys. I'm sure you already know this, but you are the most important people here today. No, I'm not joking. Scooping is serious business. You don't want the Nana Knitters to be slipping in poo, do you? Contrary to the song, we don't want Grandma to be run over by, well, a marching band in this case, but you get the drift? Good. Now, make sure to keep one hand clean for cookies. We don't want any cross contamination."

Then she loaded up their pockets with sugar cookies and sent them out the door. She side-eyed the one remaining cookie on the tray and debated for about a second before snatching it up and taking a bite. She held it in her mouth as she shrugged on her coat and shut off the lights.

"Father Christmas," she said more in her head than out loud since her mouth was stuffed with cookie, "if I'm not too old for a wish...please let today go well."

She stepped outside into brilliant morning sunshine. It reflected off yesterday's snowfall, creating a silvery mirror all around them. Caroline tugged the sunglasses from her pocket and slid them on. Cold air chilled her nose as she took a deep breath, but it wasn't enough to be freezing.

"It's going to be a beautiful day, people." She reached her car at the curb and opened the door. "A beautiful day."

The team piled into three vehicles and drove to the staging area in Tin Soldier General Store's parking lot. A mass of people already stood outside the store's door waiting for direction. Caroline parked at the far back of the lot so the floats and paradees would have enough room to assemble. She stepped out and rolled her shoulders back.

Today she showed them all they did the right thing electing her. She wouldn't let the town down. And most importantly, she wouldn't let herself down.

"I was made for this." She told herself and strode towards the crowd of people. "I am in control."

She stopped in front of the group, and her team fanned out around her. She raised her arm in the air and glanced both ways. Several of the guys rolled their eyes and sighed but raised their arms in the air with her. All together, they shook their wrists, filling the air with the tinkle of bells. Everyone stopped talking and turned to them, their faces lit with excitement.

"Good morning, y'all" Caroline called out. "Most of you know who I am, but for those who don't, I'm Mayor Caroline Davenport. Welcome to our 97th annual Christmas kick-off parade."

The crowd clapped as Caroline paused. She'd practiced this speech in the mirror more times than she'd like to admit. Honestly, she'd practiced all of today more times than she'd ever admit to anyone. Only her husband witnessed her late-night planning sessions, which he lovingly described as 'neurotic' and 'obsessive.' Didn't matter to her. She'd do whatever it took to make sure today was a success. Reverence Ridge depended on these few weeks of tourism over the holidays to get them through the rest of the year. To say it was a big deal was an understatement.

"What a beautiful day to kick off the season, am I right? Father Christmas answered a few wishes for this perfect weather I think." She paused to smile. And breathe. "All of you should have chosen a group leader. If all the leaders will come see my assistant Presley, she'll be getting you in order for the parade."

"What about Santa?" someone called out. "Is it true Chris turned in his hat?"

"That is true." Caroline paused again to let everyone get out their surprised whispers. "Not only did he turn in his hat, but he also shaved off his beard as a symbolic gesture of a new beginning, so if you do see him, you probably won't recognize him. But if you do recognize him, congratulate him on his 32 years as a successful town Santa."

"So, who's ending the parade?" someone else hollered.

"Thank you for asking. I have a short list here of gentlemen interested in the position, if there's anyone else who'd like to put their name in the hat, come see me. I'll make the decision shortly." She paused, but then added, "These are some big boots to fill, gentlemen. Uncle Chris was a heck of a Santa. So don't apply if you're not up to the job. Oh, and a fake beard is supplied but I hear it's rather itchy. So, be prepared for a few weeks' worth of yearly chin itch if you can't grow your own."

"Wow, boss. Way to sell it." Presley whistled as they broke off to get started.

"The whole point was to scare away the applicants who aren't serious about the job. I mean, it's Santa. The job isn't easy, so we need someone dedicated and I don't have time to weed through people this morning."

"Good call." Presley saluted Caroline with her pen. "I'll get started on our line-up."

"Whew!" Caroline jingled her bracelet and wiggled her hips. "Let's do this."

"Mommy!"

Caroline spun around and was instantly crushed in a hug. A hug that barely reached her waist and shoved her back a step or two.

"Whoa." She laughed. "There's my Dancing Queens. And the big Dancer Man."

"You know I've asked you not to call me that." Her husband leaned over the kids to hug her. "Especially in public."

"There is no shame in Dancer Man."

"The whole town doesn't need to know I like to bust a move every now and then."

"So, every day all day is 'every now and then,' huh?"

"Hey. It makes the cleaning go faster, ok?"

"And entertains the rest of us at the same time. The Floss you busted out yesterday while doing the dishes was particularly impressive."

"Shhh." He glanced around making sure no one heard, but she could feel him smile when he leaned in to kiss her cheek.

Caroline knelt and wrapped her twin girls up in her arms. She sighed into their hair after seeing the outfits under their unzipped coats. Zoey was in a lovely mixture of red plaid on top and neon floral pants. Cloe at least had on a Christmas dress. From last year. It was no longer a dress, but a too tight shirt with jeans underneath. While she had a 'give-them-a-couple-parent-approved-choices' philosophy when it came to clothing, her darling husband, Joe, had a 'let-them-express-themselves-no-matter-what' attitude. But today, as long as they were happy, that's all that mattered.

"Oh, Mommy needed that hug this morning." She squeezed them before stepping back and patting their hair.

"Whoa." Zoey ducked and pushed her hand away.

"Yeah, hands off the 'do, Mom." Cloe chimed in.

"I apologize." Caroline said.

"Daddy practiced today."

"And he's getting better."

"So, hands off." They both said together. Then they spotted Jim's boys with the scoopers and bolted in that direction, pigtails streaming out behind them.

"Geez. Five going on fifteen." Caroline leaned into Joe and snuggled in under his arm. "You did good though. Like, real good."

"I have been getting a lot of practice lately."

"I know. I'm sorry. We just have to get through today."

"I didn't say that to make you feel bad." He squeezed her tighter, ruffling her hair with one hand. "I'm really proud of you. You're doing an amazing job."

Caroline pulled out from under his arm and swatted his stomach. Then she quickly smoothed her hair back into place.

"Thank you. It's nice to hear that. Especially today."

"You got this."

"I know," she tisked. She glanced at her phone and saw that it was 9 o'clock. "Ok. It's go time. We have to get this show on the road. Literally."

"Girls," Joe called. "Let's go."

They returned the scoopers to the boys and raced back.

"Why don't we get to be scoopers, Mommy?" Cloe asked with her hands on her hips.

"I thought you wanted to watch the parade, sweetie."

"No. We want to be in it." Cloe scowled.

"You get to help. Why can't we?" Zoey asked.

"Well, this is Mommy's job now. I have to make sure everything is running smoothly because this parade is important to our town."

"If it's your job, then it's our job."

"We can be scoopers too. I want cookies."

"Oh, my sweets. I don't have any jobs left. Maybe next year when you're a little bigger..." Caroline stopped, knowing she'd crossed a line.

"Bigger? You tell us every day you can't believe how big we are."

"Um, help," Caroline whispered to Joe through the corner of her mouth.

"Yeah, Mommy. We are so big we can totally scoop poop."

"Alright my ladies. I do not want you anywhere near poop." Joe put a hand on each of their shoulders. "The car would stink for days, and I don't want to smell poop on the way to Nana's for Christmas dinner. What would Papa say when we walked in stinking of poo?"

The girls bent their heads together and whispered furiously for approximately five seconds before looking back at Caroline and crossing their arms.

"Fine. We won't scoop poop."

"But only because we know Papa has a sensitive nose." Zoey wiggled her nose in sympathy. "Member he hated that perfume you wore last year?"

"What?" Caroline asked. "Me? My perfume?"

"Ok girls, I think we'll go find a place to watch the parade." Joe ushered them towards the sidewalk.

"You never told me he didn't like my perfume." Caroline called after them. "He bought me that perfume."

"Text me when you can come join us." Joe waved over his shoulder. "We'll be waiting for you."

"Hurry up, Mommy."

"We'll save you a spot."

Caroline threw her hands up and let them hit her thighs when they fell. She glanced at her phone again. 9:05. Shoot. She should have been huddled up with a group of Santa wannabes by now. She flipped over her clipboard and hustled towards the crowd.

"Alright, I need my Santa applicants over here ASAP." She pointed to the area she stood in. "Presley, how's line-up?"

"Moving right along, Mrs. Mayor."

Caroline shot her a thumbs up and added a jingle of the wrist for spice. Then she turned back to the group that had gathered around her. She'd had three names on her list from the town meeting. Now, she had six men in front of her. So much for the face itch threat scaring them off.

She really needed to step up for this decision. It could make or break the holiday season. She shuddered when she thought of Holly Oaks down the highway and their Santa incident several years ago. A Santa who's severely allergic to pine trees does not a good Santa make. Holly Oaks's holiday festivities still hadn't recovered.

"I'm going to try to make this as quick and painless as possible. How about you all get in a line to make this simpler." She paused as they all moved onto one of the painted parking spot lines. "I'll be asking each of you each a series of questions. Please answer honestly and quickly. We're in a time crunch, gentlemen."

She checked her clipboard as she walked down the line of applicants. Stew from the bank. Nolan from the Post Office. Greg who was retired military. Charlie who owned the General Store. And Pat their local mechanic. Then she arrived at the last applicant. He straightened his shoulders and pulled himself up as tall as he could, but he still only reached Caroline's shoulders.

"Well, hello there, Chuck." Caroline let the clipboard fall to her side.

"Hey, Mrs. Davenport." Chuck squeaked.

"Now, I'd love to interview you, but you're not old enough to work. Why are you even trying to apply?"

"Lifelong job security, ma'am." Chuck nodded seriously. "My mama's always talkin' about how important job security is. And what could be more secure than Santa? He'll never go out of style."

"Well, thank you for your interest. Come back and see me in four years when you turn eighteen and we'll see what we can do."

"Really?" Chucks face lit up. He grabbed Caroline's hand and shook it vigorously. "Thank you, ma'am."

Caroline shook her head and chuckled to herself as he ran off on his gangly legs. Her phone buzzed in her hand. She had it set to emergency contacts only, so that left two options. Her mother, who was on a cruise in the Bahamas. Or Joe.

J: Hey, Darlin.

J: We got a spot in front of Wizzle's.

J: The girls are going nuts.

J: I'm not sure we'll last until the parade starts.

Caroline looked back down the line of men in front of her and sighed. She'd promised the girls, and Joe, that as soon as the parade was off and running, she'd join them to watch. Presley and a few others on the team who didn't have kids said they'd be happy to ensure the end of the parade went off without a hitch.

That had been the plan. Until their beloved Santa quit last night and now the entire end of the parade, the most anticipated part, was all up in the air. And so were her plans with the girls. She really didn't want to disappoint them or leave Joe high and dry. As she walked back to the first applicant, she realized this would be harder than she thought.

Stew Lancaster, the bank branch manager, stood at attention. Like she was a drill sergeant and he a new recruit. She tapped her pen on her clipboard and pursed her lips, picturing him in a red suit and long beard. He smiled at her and waited patiently.

On her clipboard next to 'Appearance' she wrote "Santa-esque, Pass."

"Bedtime?" she asked.

"Whenever I'm tired."

"I need a time estimate please, Mr. Lancaster."

"Um. Ten o'clock."

Next to 'Night Availability' she wrote 'Acceptable. Pass'

She asked several more questions pertaining to availability, experience with kids, and dietary restrictions. She asked the same questions to each of them, writing down their answers as she went.

"Now, most importantly. I need to hear each of you 'Ho. Ho. Ho.' please."

Pat, the last in line, placed his hands on his hips and bellowed a deep, rich 'Ho. Ho. Ho.' followed with an equally jolly, belly-jiggling chuckle. Caroline nodded and wrote 'Particularly impressive' next to 'Hos.'

"Thank you, Pat. That's going to be a tough act to follow."

But as it turned out, the next four men did equally as well. She'd expected the 'Ho. Ho. Ho's' to really elevate one of them above the rest, but they all had their own takes on it that were equally holly jolly. So, that wouldn't be the determining factor for the next Reverence Ridge Santa after all.

Each was pretty outstanding, except for one factor. One had a bum knee, making it difficult for kids to sit on his lap for long. One was lactose intolerant, making milk and cookies a no-go. One had seasonal allergies, meaning if December was unseasonably warm, they'd have one stuffy, possibly snotty, Santa. One said he was asleep by eight every night, meaning evening events would have one very sleepy Santa. And one was skinnier than Charlie Brown's Christmas tree, which meant the Santa Suit would need some hefty tailoring or padding. But everything else checked out.

"Man. You guys are making it tough on me today." She smiled as her phone buzzed again.

> J: Full blown mutiny.

> J: Neighbors are glaring.

There was a pause, then another buzz.

> J: I hope the Santa hunt is going better.

> J: Go get your man!

Caroline smiled and then her phone buzzed for a third time.

> J: Send the scoopers with cookies.

> J: Momentary distraction is worth the sugar craze later.

> You sure?

> After that craze comes the crash.

> Send. The. Cookies.

> Sent.

Caroline called Jim's boys over and gave them each $5 to purchase snacks for the girls from the vendors. Their eyes lit up as she handed them the money.

"When my husband texts me the girls got their snacks, there will be another $5 for each of you when you get back." She gave them her most stern look. "But if you try to run off with that, pretty sure that'd leave you on the naughty list. Am I right boys?"

She glanced over her shoulder at the Santas. All five agreed. Stew even busted out in song.

"He knows if you've been bad or good, so be good for goodness' sake."

The boys looked at each other and took off across the parking lot.

> Scoopers are deployed.

> I repeat scoopers are deployed.

> Please verify cookie delivery.

She closed out of text and saw the time. 9:20. It really was the most magical time of the year because the minutes were just disappearing. She ran her tongue across her teeth, thinking about the Santas. There had to be something to set them apart. And there was only one person who knew what that was. She quickly shot off another text and said a prayer they'd get here in time.

"Guys. I'm going to need a few minutes. I'm sorry to make you wait here, but this is a big decision."

"No problem, boss." Nolan tipped his hat at her.

"I've got to check a few things and then I'll be back."

Caroline hurried into the crowd to find Presley. She raised her wrist and jingled every few steps. Pretty soon she'd located most of her team. Jim was on the ground underneath a float of a dog wearing a Santa hat, pulling out wires and switching plugs. As she watched, the dog suddenly started spinning and music started blaring from speakers in its ears. She smiled and gave Jim a thumbs up as he climbed out from under the float.

As she walked down the line leading out to the street, she checked them off the list in her head. She straightened a few hats, changed a few bulbs in light strands, and fixed a broken shoelace for the dance team. All the while walking around with one arm in the air jingling the bells. She was almost at the front of the line when she heard an answering jingle. Presley struggled to hold a papier mâché arm taller than she was.

Caroline rushed over and took the weight off her poor assistant. Presley sighed as the weight shifted.

"Small mechanical crisis on our front float." Presley breathlessly said. "We have a lame wizard arm."

"I don't think we should be calling names, Presley." Caroline lowered her voice and said through clenched teeth.

"No. Lame as in not functioning. The Christmas Wizard on Wizzle's float. It's his wand arm."

"Oh no, the kids love the wand arm."

"I know."

"Here, hold this." Caroline handed the arm back to Presley who grunted under the weight.

Soon, she was waist deep in a papier mâché wizards arm socket looking at gears, engines, and a very unhappy Mitchell Wizzle. His typically impeccable purple tuxedo jacket was tied around his waist like some teen's hoodie. Caroline knew at that moment it was bad.

"What can I do, Mitch?"

"Unless you're a mechanic, not much."

"A mechanic I am not, but I do happen to know Pat is here."

"Pat's here? Thank you, Father Christmas." Mitch pressed his palms together and raised them above his head.

"Presley." Caroline pulled her head out of the wizard and hollered down. "We need Pat, stat. He's over in the Santa line-up in the parking lot."

Presly, who still held the giant arm, hesitated a moment, turning one way then the other.

"I can't set this down. The ground is wet, it will damage the wand arm."

Caroline pulled the rest of her body out of the arm hole and paused for a moment. The idea crossed her mind that they could just have a message sent from float to float until it reached Pat, like the game Telephone. A message like 'Pat, we have a mechanical wizard emergency. Help!' would probably turn into something about a maniacal blizzard surgery. And the last thing she needed right now was evil weather related medical questions. So, that wouldn't work.

She glanced around again and saw the high school debate team two floats down. With two fingers in her mouth, she let out a piercing whistle. Instantly everything around her stilled.

"Alright, Ridgers, we have a wizard emergency." She pointed to the Sage horn Tree Farm float next to them. "Two of you come help poor Presley hold this thing."

Two men rushed over and took the arm from Presley, who sagged to the ground in relief.

"Jake Hernandez." She pointed to the debate team. "You run track, right?"

"Yes, ma'am." He stammered, tugging at the collar of his shirt. "Can't say I'm very good though."

"Well, beggars can't be choosers." Caroline sighed. "Run as fast as you can back to the parking lot and get Pat, the mechanic. Tell him it's an emergency."

Jake took off running, his tie flapping over his shoulder. Caroline looked at her phone. 9:35. She also saw she'd missed a text from Joe.

J: Cookie delivery confirmed.

J: Sugar rush commencing.

First Float emergency.

Detained until completed. Save my spot.

Caroline ducked back into the wizard to let Mitch know help was on the way. She offered to take his jacket to keep it from being sucked into a gear or covered with engine grease. It was wrinkled almost beyond recognition. The first float of the parade had to be on point. And Wizzle's was always a crowd pleaser, but if they couldn't get all these kinks ironed out, literally, they were in trouble. When she saw the coffee shop across the street, she had an idea.

"Sandy," she yelled at one of the women from the tree farm float. "Take this over to the coffee shop and hold it in some steam. Get out as many wrinkles as you can."

"On it, Caroline- I mean, Mayor Davenport." Sandy rushed over and took the purple jacket.

Suddenly, she heard a distant jingle of bracelet bells. With a hand over her eyes to lessen the glare, she looked down the line of floats. Another bracelet started jingling, this one a little closer. Then another. Finally, she spotted Pat speeding her way on a motor scooter. His helmet was painted like a skull and its neon pink mohawk had been covered with an elf hat, pointy ears and all.

Caroline jumped down, landing in a pile of ankle-deep snow. As she shook the cold wetness off her feet, Pat parked and threw off his helmet. She glanced at her phone.

"Pat. We have twenty minutes until the parade starts. We need this wizard's wand waving. Are you the man for the job?"

"You betcha." He ran right past her without a second glance and dove in through the arm hole.

"I have never been so glad for large wizard armpits as I am today." She mumbled to herself.

Her phone buzzed in her pocket. Joe was probably in the throes of the sugar rush by now and desperate for help. She could just imagine the glares from the people sitting next to them when she finally arrived.

And Joe, poor Joe. He had a habit of running his hands through his hair when he was stressed. He'd probably look like a Chia pet before she was done here.

> J: Not Wizzle's float?!?

> J: Your spot is safe. I wrote SAVED FOR MAYOR OF REVERENCE RIDGE on a cookie wrapper and I'm shocked people are actually respecting it.

That text was followed by another. A photo of her girls sitting on the curb. Next to them was the cookie wrapper holding her spot. A strong tug twisted her stomach. She should be there with them, making memories. But she also needed to be here. Not just wanted, needed. She'd wanted to be mayor of this town since she was ten years old. Strange dream for a kid, but it was hers. And she was finally here doing a knock-out job, if she did say so herself.

"I was made for this. I am in control." She took a deep breath.

"Control is just an illusion, dear. Better to let go of it now."

She turned around to see her Aunt Birdie, who wrapped her in a quick squeeze. Her Uncle Chris, almost unrecognizable without his signature long, white beard, stood next to her aunt smiling.

"Looks like you've got everything running smoothly here." He nodded.

"Well, then looks are deceiving. Because I have a waveless wizard, a line-up of Santa wannabes who would all be good, but I have to decide who would be the best. Oh, and I have a family who's waiting for me. I thought I could do it all. Be mom and mayor. Maybe I was wrong."

Uncle Chris stepped forward and put an arm around her shoulders. He tipped her face up with a finger under her chin.

"Life is all a balance. Sometimes that takes some time to find, but it looks to me like you're doing just fine."

"Tell that to my little girls sitting on the curb with an empty cookie wrapper taking the place of their mother." She shoved her phone into his face and then sighed.

"What if this was just a pipe dream, Uncle Chris? I mean, am I really cut out to lead this town? Especially at Christmas? This town relies on these few weeks to get through the rest of the year. If I blow it this year, that could affect us for years to come. We might never make a comeback. Look at Holly Oaks."

"You're spiraling, dear." Aunt Birdie came up on her other side and wrapped an arm around her waist. "You've wanted this job your whole life. And you've finally got it. You won your election by a landslide. This whole town *knows* you can do this job. Now you need to start believing it, too."

"You know what?" Caroline sniffled and wiped her nose. "You're right. I did win by a landslide. I mean, that wasn't hard with the competition, but still. I'll take it."

"There's that quirky fire we love." Birdie smiled.

"Ok. We have a Santa situation." Caroline turned fully to her uncle. "Last night, I thought we wouldn't have any Santa. Now we have too many."

She went over the situation with her uncle, who, up until last night, had been the town Santa for over thirty years. He listened intently, his care and love for the job still written all over his freshly shaven face.

"How do I choose? How do I pick the right one?" She threw her hands up.

"I'm going to tell you the most important thing about this job." Chris put his arm through hers and the started walking back past the floats. "It's about the kids. For the kids. That's it. It's that simple."

"That's it? It's simple?" She asked, slightly exasperated by her uncle's habit of oversimplifying. "So, what am I supposed to do with that?"

"I'm not sure, but I know you'll sort it out." Chris patted her arm. "Now, we need to go find a spot to watch. Us old folks don't move as fast anymore."

Caroline looked in one direction and saw four guys milling around in a slush covered parking lot, waiting for her decision. In the other direction, an armless wizard. As she stared, Pat crawled out the arm hole. He hollered something back inside and made a circling motion with his hand. Caroline held her breath. The sound of an engine revving was better than the most festive Christmas carol she'd ever heard. A cheer went up around her as all the paradees raised their arms and clapped. Pat turned and took a bow from the float before helping Mitch crawl out the arm hole he just came from. With the help from the Sagehorn men, they got the arm in place and attached in no time.

Caroline glanced at her phone. 9:45. Once she unlocked it, she saw the picture of her girls again. At five years old, they were at the perfect age for Christmas. They were young enough to believe in all the magic and wonder, and they were old enough that they could understand it all. She thought back to that morning when they were so ready to help. It brought a smile to her face and an idea to her mind.

> Love the cookie wrapper.

> Leave it. Bring the girls. I found them a job.

After a moment of thought she added a second text.

> ASAP. Meet me where you left me this morning.

Before heading back to the parking lot, she returned to Presley and the Wizzle's wizard, who's wand arm was waving and blowing bubbles. That was new this year. She climbed up onto the float, dodging the wand and whistled again. Everyone around her turned to look once more.

"Alright, Ridgers. Our wizard is back, and we are almost ready to launch this parade. This will be our best one yet. Keep those smiles on and let's spread some holiday cheer." She hopped down while everyone hooted and cheered. "Presley, you're in charge of the parade kick-off. I have to go settle our Santa situation."

"Ay, ay, Captain." Presley saluted and turned on her heel.

"Can I give you a lift?" Pat asked from behind her. He wore his skull elf helmet and held out one for her.

"That'd be wonderful. Thank you." She hopped onto the scooter behind him, and they zoomed past floats and around slush piles.

"I have to tell you; I scrubbed and scrubbed my hands this morning to come see you about the Santa job." He hollered over his shoulder as the wind whipped past. He briefly held up one hand, smeared with black, for her to see. "And now here I am covered in oil and grease again."

They stopped next to the other Santa candidates and slid off the scooter. Caroline handed him the helmet and fluffed her hair.

"Yes, thank you so much for you help. You saved the parade." She smiled. "Don't think I can use that to give you an edge here though."

"That's what I wanted to talk to you about." He looked down and scuffed his feet. "I love kids and I love Christmas, but I'm more of an under the hood kind of guy. People cheering for me up on that float wasn't my kind of thing. So, I'll take my name out of the hat for the position if that's ok with you."

"You would make a wonderful Santa, but I totally understand."

She heard the sound of running feet behind her and turned just as her girls plowed into her legs. Joe walked up next with an outstretched cup of coffee. Caroline snatched it and gulped down half of it instantly.

"How did you get here so fast?" she asked.

"We were already on our way back to see if you needed any help." Joe smiled and knelt next to Cloe and Zoey. "The girls said it wouldn't be any fun without you anyway."

"Aww."

"We did leave the cookie wrapper, so your spot may still be there." Joe shrugged.

"Ha. Well, I don't think we're going to need it." Caroline rubbed her hands together in anticipation. "Girls, I have a job for you."

Both Cloe and Zoey squealed and clasped their hands.

"Do you see those four guys over there? Do you know any of them?"

"Um. Not really." Cloe said.

"Good. There won't be any bias." Caroline nodded.

"What?" Zoey scrunched her nose and looked up at her.

"Now, this is a super, super important job. Can you take it seriously?" she narrowed her eyes at them.

"Yes, Mommy."

"What is it? Just tell us."

"I need you to go talk to them." Caroline crossed her arms.

"That's it?" they asked.

"That's it."

They looked at each other, shrugged, and then started skipping over. Caroline leaned into Joe and watched as they approached the Santas. They had broken up into groups of two, talking. Caroline was far enough away that they hadn't spotted her through all the other people, but she still had a clear view. Cloe approached one set of Santas, and Zoey approached the other.

One set, the guys both looked down and said hello, then returned to their conversations.

In the other group, Stew stooped down and started talking to Cloe. Soon, Zoey gravitated towards them, and both were talking very animatedly while Stew laughed.

"And there's my answer." She heaved a sigh.

"Are you going to tell me what's going on here?" Joe threw his arm over her shoulder as they started walking towards the girls.

"I just found our Santa."

"Ahhhh. Smart." Joe nodded and gave her a quick kiss on the nose. "That's my girl."

"Well, Uncle Chris said this job was all about the kids. So, who better to find our new Santa than kids?" Caroline shrugged but couldn't help the self-satisfied smile on her face. "Could you do me a favor and grab the garment bag out of the car?"

"Ohhh...the Santa suit." Joe tapped his fingers together and wiggled his eyebrows. "On it."

"Mommy, Mr. Stew said they used to use real socks for stockings." Zoey said when they approached the group.

"Only the clean ones." Stew pointed at them, making the girls giggle.

"Well, Stew, you have passed the final test. I'd like to officially offer you the position of Reverence Ridge's very own town Santa. What do you say we get you suited up and in the float before it takes off without you?"

"Oh, thank you, Caroline- I mean, Mayor Davenport. I won't let you down. Just wait until Roxie hears about this. She won't believe it."

Stew stepped aside to call his wife while Caroline thanked the other three men for their time. Then she turned back to her family with a smile.

"Thank you so much, girls. You did your job perfectly."

"That was too easy, Mommy."

"Yeah, we want to actually work. Like the scoopers."

"Well, I think that can be arranged." She laughed. "And speaking of the scoopers..."

She looked around and waved them over. They came running, their scoopers clanging on the ground with every step.

"I believe I owe you guys $5 for getting my girls their cookies. Thanks for that. Now, get up there behind the park rangers and stay in front of the Nanas. Keep the poop off the streets and I'll have a special place in the office that's always stocked with cookies for you."

Their faces lit up and they ran back up to their place in the line-up. She prayed a year supply of cookies was enough to keep them focused, and they didn't end up with horse poop tracked down Main Street. Caroline glanced down at her phone. 9:55. The front floats would start moving in minutes. She found Stew, still on the phone.

"Mr. Lancaster, it's now or never."

"Gotta go, Roxie. Watch for me at the end of the parade." Stew smiled ear to ear.

Joe arrived just then, out of breath, but with the garment bag. Stew took it and disappeared behind Santa's float to slip into the suit. Caroline opened a hatch on the float and pulled out a box. Then she called the girls over.

"Since you did so great with your last job, I have one that's just as important. And probably more fun."

She pulled four hats from the box, all different colors and styles, but each had big, pointy elf ears. The girls' eyes got big when they saw the different colors of tinsel hair. Joe didn't look quite as excited, but when he pulled on a lovely blue one, his hair flip could have rivaled any supermodel. Cloe went with green and Zoey with red, which left Caroline with silver.

"So, is that what I have to look forward to when you get old and gray?" Joe ran his hands through her tinsel with a smirk. "Cause I'm here for it."

"Let's hope that's at least a few years off." Caroline shuddered at the thought. "But with this job, I'll probably go gray before the year's out."

Caroline handed out red aprons to the whole family and they were working on tying them around each other's waists when Stew stepped out around the float. The red velvet suit fit him perfectly, like it was made to be his. The boots on the other hand were far too big and slapped the ground as he walked over to them. Besides the waddle, he was a picture-perfect Santa, down to the white fur cuffs on his sleeves and pants.

"Well, I'll be." Caroline exclaimed. "We have a perfect Santa, right down to the twinkle in his eye."

"Ho. Ho. Ho. Thanks, Mayor Davenport." Stew held his belly and chuckled, fully in the role.

"Mr. Stew, is that you?" Cloe took a cautious step towards him.

"Not when I put this suit on. I work for the Big Man himself now." Stew winked.

"You work for Santa?" Zoey stood frozen, shocked, but the tilt of her head said she was skeptical.

"Well, he needs a little extra help this time of year. What with making toys for all the good girls and boys. And making his list and checking it twice."

"Yeah, he's a busy man." Cloe elbowed Zoey.

"Everyone needs a little help at Christmas." Caroline hugged both girls to her. "Even me. Think you can do this one last job?"

"Sure."

"You betcha."

Caroline looked down at her phone. 10:05. The front floats were already making their way down Main Street. It was time to get Santa in place.

"Great. Let's get Santa in his sleigh. It's time to move." Caroline ushered the whole group of Santa and tinsel-haired elves towards the float.

The team had worked hard on updating Santa's sleigh this year. It had a fresh coat of red paint. The reindeer all sported new reins, studded with silver jingle bells that made the most beautiful tinkling sound as they float drove down the road. All of that sat on a bed of white, fluffy clouds, studded with twinkling star lights.

Joe helped Santa up into the sleigh. Caroline assured him they'd get new boots that very afternoon. It would not be good to have Santa tripping over his own feet. Once he was settled, he picked up the silver bell to ring as they drove down through town.

"Now, it's time for our job." Caroline handed each elf a bucket stuffed with candy canes.

"Oh, eating candy?" Zoey licked her lips.

"No, silly." Caroline ruffled her tinsel hair as they walked to the front of the float. "To spread Christmas cheer."

The floats in front of them began to move and they followed. Caroline leaned into Joe, spitting tinsel out of her face when he tugged her in for a hug. He did another supermodel hair flip, and she tried again. As the entered Main Street, they watched their two girls pass out the candy canes to all the children. Light radiated from them, and not just from their tinsel hair.

"Well, Mrs. Mayor," Joe whispered into her elf ear, "you did it."

"What can I say? I was made for this. I am in control."

Taylor

T aylor leaned against the door of his company truck; his last name emblazoned on the side. Callaway Contracting. Founded by his great, great grandfather, Wilmer Callaway, in 1872. And his birthright.

His breath hung in the early morning air. He shivered in his light jacket even though he'd layered with a thermal undershirt and button-down flannel. Come afternoon, he'd probably shed two of the three layers. Hard work had a way of warming you up, no matter the weather.

Muted orange and pink sunlight was barely shining over the Smoky Mountains that surrounded the town. The streets were still empty, but Mindy was kind enough to open Cup of Cheer early for his guys to get their morning caffeine and sugar fix. While the crew sat inside, in the warmth and light, he soaked in his last moments of peace and sipped at the caramel hazelnut latte in his Darth Vader mug. The guys ragged on him when he ordered it, but this was the only time of year he could get it. And, dang, if it wasn't delicious.

"How ya doin', boss?" Kenny walked out of the coffee shop and stuffed his hands in his pockets.

"How many times have I told you not to call me that?" Taylor tossed back the last of his coffee and set his mug inside on the dash with his collection of other coffee cups in varying states of cleanliness.

"But the other guys get to," Kenny jokingly whined with a smile.

"Those other guys haven't been my best friend since kindergarten." Taylor shook his head and sighed.

"Seriously though, you alright, man?" Kenny cleared his throat. "You're standing out here in the cold all by yourself at the crack of dawn. What gives?"

"Just needed some quiet before today."

"Yeah, it's a big one."

"Uh Huh. First year Dad's sitting this one out." Taylor scrubbed at the scruff on his cheeks. "Kinda feels like this is a test or something."

"Ha. I wouldn't put it past your old man to come spy on us. You know, peeking around cars and whatnot?"

Taylor snorted. He could totally see his dad doing that. 'Just checking in' he'd say. And Taylor, like always, would have to remind him that 'checking in' didn't involve sneaking and ninja moves.

"What time is Big Bertha supposed to get here?"

"0900." Taylor checked his watch. "Tell the guys they've got about ten more minutes then we need to get moving."

"Right on, bo..." Kenny stopped when Taylor's eyes narrowed.

Taylor slid into the driver seat of his truck, rubbing his hands together and blowing on them for warmth. He rubbed a silver coin hanging from the rearview mirror, his good luck charm from the All-State Championship game his senior year. It's surface was almost worn smooth after all these years. He hopped out stared up as the last stars faded from the sky.

"Time to get to work."

Taylor glanced both ways, even though there was no traffic in the town square yet, and walked across the road to the city park. On the far end of the green space stood the gazebo surrounded by Frasier Firs, which they'd decked out with lights and oversized ornaments last week. Today, they'd be focusing on the closest part of the park, a large, open expanse of ground the folks of Reverence Ridge fondly called the Field of Festivities. In the summer, it held their Fourth of July Picnic. It'd seen countless weddings, anniversaries, birthdays, and county fairs. But at Christmas, it really earned its name. Today, it'd be where they'd ground Big Bertha, the forty-five-foot Norway Spruce that was, at that moment, riding into town on a semi-trailer.

They had the whole process pretty well orchestrated. Years ago, it'd started with pullies and rope, and now relied on the crane and boom truck his father had purchased specifically for this job. Not that they didn't have other opportunities to bust out the crane, but this was its main function every year.

Taylor heard boots pounding the earth behind him and turned to his crew. There were ten of them, all hands on deck today.

"Alright guys, most of you know the drill today. For the couple of you who don't, I'll give you assignments shortly. Thanks for giving up your Sunday to come into work. The town appreciates it, and so do I. There wouldn't be a tree lighting tonight without all of you."

Kenny began clapping the other guys on the back trying to get them fired up. Taylor, who could only muster the energy for necessities at this time of day, waited patiently for the guys to settle back down.

"Kenny, take two guys with the boom truck to get the tether anchors in place." He turned in a circle, pointing at store rooftops. "There, there, and there."

Kenny broke off with one of their veteran workers and one of the newbies. That left Taylor and six guys for the rest of the work.

"The rest of us will be breaking up into two teams. I'll be working on the tree base with one of you, the rest will be building the scaffolding to place around the base. Let's get moving."

Taylor took the other new guy and left the rest to get started. Taylor looked at his watch and glanced down the street just as the mayor's car tore into a parking spot across from the field. A woman tumbled out of the car, her dark hair pulled into a messy bun, strands flying out as she ran across the field. She hugged a long white trench coat to her stomach, but Taylor grinned when he saw the flannel pajama pants sticking out the bottom.

"Am I late?" She put a hand on Taylor's shoulder for support and leaned over to catch her breath. "I'm sorry. My alarm…"

"You're right on time, Mrs. Mayor." Taylor couldn't help the humor in his voice.

"Ugh. It's too early for that. Just call me Caroline."

"So, you have the key, Caroline?"

"Do I have the key?" Caroline asked jokingly, but then started patting her pockets frantically. "Oh brother, do I have the key?"

Taylor crossed his arms and rocked back on his heels, waiting.

"A-ha!" Caroline pulled a large golden key from her pocket. "I *do* have the key."

She handed it to Taylor, who took hold of the metal reindeer keychain it dangled from. They walked to the center of the field, the thin layer of icy snow crunching under their feet. A metal door, edged in a ring of concrete was built into the ground. Taylor used the keychain to chip ice off the padlock on the door before inserting the key. He had to apply some muscle before it finally turned with a satisfying click.

"Phew." Caroline laughed and patted Taylor's bicep. "Glad that was you and not me."

"That was nothing." Taylor flexed the arm closest to her. "Next, we get to open this ridiculously thick metal door, which is probably more frozen than the lock was. Oh, and then we'll move around a three to four-thousand-pound tree. So, think I could skip the gym today?"

"I give you my mayoral pardon." She waved her hand like she held a magic wand." But seriously. You guys are phenomenal. I don't know how you do this every year. It seems monumental and unfathomable to me, yet you still do it."

"It's our pleasure, ma'am." Jeremy, the newbie, stepped forward with a smile.

"Well, I'll get out of your hair." Caroline smiled back. "Don't forget we'll have a nice warm lunch for all of you over at Mistle Tomes."

"Skye's been talking about it every day this week. I don't think I *could* forget it. She'd come out and drag us all in there."

"Well, do you blame her?" Caroline looked around and lowered her voice, even though the park was deserted except for the crew. "Getting to break in that new kitchen you built her is exciting. She's been dreaming of it for years. So, get excited."

Caroline poked him in the chest with those last words. Then she hugged her coat tighter around her body and stamped her feet.

"Is the mayor's job done here? I gotta get home to feed the girls. And Joe." When Taylor nodded, Caroline turned and hollered at the rest of the crew with a final wave, "You guys are amazing. I can't wait to see Bertha in all her glory."

The guys hollered back farewells as she hustled to her car. She backed out a lot slower than she'd flown into the spot. Taylor turned his attention back to the metal door at his feet.

"Alright, Jer, let's get this open."

Taylor nodded towards the top of the door for Jer to grab. Together, they got a few fingers under it, but the center was frozen shut and wouldn't budge, no matter how much muscle they threw at it.

"'Work smarter', as the old man would say." Taylor let the door fall back down. "I'll be right back."

He jogged over and opened the toolbox in the bed of his truck. A tangled mass of cords, straps, and wire that he'd been meaning to organize laid on top. Just as he'd pulled it all out to sort through the tools at the bottom, he heard tires crunching in the parking spot next to him. Everleigh, one of the mail carriers, waved as she pulled up in her mail truck packed to the brim with letters and packages.

"Hey, Taylor," She called through the door.

When she stepped out of the truck, Taylor saw she hadn't broken her strike against the postal service uniform. She had on a necklace of blinking Christmas lights, an ear flap hat with a glittery pom-pom, and felt elf shoe covers over her boots.

"Everleigh, festive as always."

"You know it. Gotta add the fun to functional."

"You're out awful early. And on a Sunday?" Taylor turned back to his truck and began sifting through the pile of tools again.

"Volunteered to help us stay on top of things. Busiest time of the year, and all. But I'm here to see you actually."

"I don't really have time this morning. We're also really busy."

"Well, I won't take long. I promise," Everleigh said in a sing-song voice. "I have something for you."

"Can't presents wait until tomorrow?" Taylor hung his head and sighed.

"Oh, I didn't realize we were exchanging gifts." Everleigh's shoes jingled as she fidgeted. "I haven't gotten you anything...yet. But we can for sure exchange tomorrow."

"Not necessary, Everleigh." Taylor chuckled and turned to look at her. "What have you got?"

"Oh, you got a letter." She turned to dig through the bag in her car. "Of the secret variety."

Taylor's breath hitched in his chest. His hand felt like it would tremor, but he held it steady as he reached out. Everleigh slid it into his hand, writing side down, and winked.

"Good luck," she said as she slid back into her truck. When she started the engine, the local morning radio show blared from the speakers.

Everleigh pulled out and waved to Taylor, who hadn't moved yet. He couldn't get his eyes to focus as he considered the possibilities in his hand. He debated waiting to open it. He didn't need any distractions on the biggest day of the year for their company. He set the letter on the driver seat of his truck and turned back to the pile of tools.

"Oh, who am I kidding?"

He hopped into the cab of the truck and flipped the letter over. Smoky Mountain University emblazoned the envelope in an icy blue, an outline of the mountains in the background. There in the center, was his name. Taylor Callaway. He took a deep breath and tore into the envelope.

We'd like to congratulate you on your acceptance to SMU. Your previous status on the wait list has been changed. You are now eligible to start classes in January, 2022.

Please contact our student aid and scheduling departments to complete your enrollment.

Again, congratulations. And welcome to the SMU family. Go Mountaineers!

Taylor folded the letter and laid it in his lap. As he stared out the windshield, the passenger door swung open, and someone slid inside. Taylor quickly tried to fold the letter and stuff it in the envelope.

"Whoa. Calm down, man. What is that?" Kenny craned his neck to see. "SMU. Do they have a gig for us or something?"

"No. This isn't about the company." Taylor continued to stare forward but handed the letter to his friend.

"Dude. Congrats. I thought you gave up on college years ago." Kenny pounded Taylor's shoulder.

"It's just a pipe dream." Taylor finally tore his eyes away from the brick wall in front of them. "I applied last summer and got wait-listed. So, thought that dream was over again."

"Obviously not." Kenny handed the letter back. "So, are you going to go?"

"How am I supposed to? I can't just pack up and leave for four years."

"Man, SMU was your dream back in high school. You finally got accepted. If that isn't like the best Christmas gift ever, I don't know what is." Kenny had a goofy smile and was nodding vigorously. "You have to go."

"Yeah, Ken, I just don't know." Taylor scrubbed his face with both hands. "You can't tell anyone about this. Not until I make a decision."

"Of course. Of course."

"Thanks, man." Taylor pushed out along breath. "Let's get back out there. Bertha will be here soon. And Randy should be rolling up with the crane any minute."

After more digging through the toolbox, Taylor found a crowbar. Kenny grabbed a socket set and headed back to the rooftops. People were pulling in for coffee before church service, so traffic was starting to pick up. Taylor nodded at a few family friends as he jogged back to the field. By the time he arrived, his breath came out in puffs.

"Ok, Jer, let's get this open."

With the crowbar wedged in the middle and Jeremy pulling from the top, the door finally flew open, falling to the ground with a clang. They both lifted the other side and looked down into the hole. It was about four feet deep, concrete on all sides. In the center of the floor, a smaller hole, about two inches in diameter, was surrounded with a ring of industrial eyebolts along the outside.

Taylor hopped down into the hole to inspect all the bolts, making sure they were all intact and not rusted, but the metal door was so thick and well made that very little water ever made it into the hole.

"So, you coming out with the guys tonight?" Jer hopped down in next to him, watching and mimicking what he was doing on the opposite side. "Maybe enjoy a little eggnog?"

"Ha!" Taylor couldn't help but laugh. "I wouldn't drink eggnog if you paid me $100."

"Is it the brandy? Cause if you don't like that, try it with a good ol' Tennessee bourbon."

"It's not the booze." Taylor heard a distant rumble and looked over to the street. "It's the damn nutmeg. Come on, I hear Randy coming."

"Oh yeah. I remember something about you being allergic. And a nickname you got? What was it?" Jeremy laughed hesitantly. "Oh yeah. Prancer."

"Not sure what people expect you to do when your eyes swell shut, and you keep ramming your shins into everything." Taylor mumbled as he pulled himself up onto the side of the hole. "So, yeah, I'm sure I walked a little funny."

Jeremy just snickered as he hopped up on the side as well.

"Let's just not mention that. Especially this time of year." Taylor shuddered, remembering the plethora of reindeer jokes he'd been the butt of.

The two of them hopped up and hurried across the field as a large crane came into view. When they'd first bought it, they had it painted a powder blue to match their company logo. On cloudless mornings, like it was just then, the boom blended in perfectly with the sky. Taylor always liked that it didn't obstruct the view, because in a scenic place like Reverence Ridge, views were important.

"Ran-dy," Jeremy hooted over the sound of the engine.

Randy waved from inside the cab as he moved a few levers and the crane lurched to a halt. He pulled on his coat and hopped out to the ground.

"Morning." Randy spit a few sunflower shells onto the ground. "Made it before Bertha, huh?"

"Yep. She'll be here any minute, and we can get this show on the road." Taylor kicked his boot against the crane's tire. "Got the base for us?"

"Sure do. On the back."

Strapped onto the backend of the crane, Taylor and Jeremy found the two pieces for the Christmas tree base. Each piece was a half-circle that stood about two feet high and had bolts spaced about every six inches sticking out the bottom. Jeremy and Taylor each grabbed one and threw it over their shoulders.

"This thing weighs like a hundred pounds, boss." Jeremy huffed and adjusted the weight more evenly on his back.

"What did you expect to hold up a three-thousand-pound tree? One of those dainty little tree stands you find at Walmart?" Taylor situated his a little better and strode across the grass. "And don't call me boss."

Over the next twenty minutes, they bolted the bases into the eye-bolts at the bottom of the hole, as well as bolting them together to form a solid circle for the trunk to rest in. By the time they'd finished, the sun was fully shining in the sky, and Taylor had chucked off his jacket.

"Hey, Jer, go help the guys with the scaffolding, would ya?" Kenny jumped down into the hole as Taylor was tightening the last bolt. He dragged a massive extension cord behind him.

"The tether anchors done?" Taylor asked as he wiped his brow with the back of his hand.

"Sure are. Got the wire anchored to the rooftops. Even twisted the big bulb lights around them to save us time later." Kenny twisted the extension cord around the base to hold it in place. "So, are you going to tell your dad about SMU?"

"Definitely not today. But yeah. At some point I suppose I'll have to tell the old man."

"Tell me what?" a gruff voice asked from above and behind him.

Taylor shook his head, but turned to face his father, who was silhouetted against the sun. Using a hand to shield his eyes, he squinted against the light.

"You got something to tell me, son, you better do it now before Bertha gets here." His father made no move.

"Sorry, Bro." Kenny patted his shoulder and vaulted out of the hole. "I'm gonna leave you to it."

"Gee, thanks," Taylor said as he hauled himself out of the hole. He stood next to his father, both with their hands in the pockets staring down into the hole. "What are you doin' here, Dad?"

"Brought your mother for some of those biscuit-y things she likes for breakfast. The skinny, crunchy ones you dunk in coffee." His lip curled in distaste. "What's wrong with muffins? Or pancakes? Or things you don't have to sog up to avoid breaking a tooth on?"

Taylor knew his father was avoiding the conversation, but Taylor didn't have time for this dance today. Better to look at it like a band-aid. Just rip it off and get it over with.

"I applied to SMU for their business program," he said. "I got wait listed in August and figured that was the end of it. Then I got a letter this morning that a spot opened up and I could start next month."

He held his breath and waited for his father's response.

"Was going to ask you to come sit with us for a moment. Eat something. I know you think coffee counts as breakfast, but you are wrong, son."

"Dad. I don't have time to sit down for biscotti and coffee." That was not the response he'd expected. "Did you hear what I said? I'd have to leave for four years, but I think..."

"Come sit down, son." His father turned on the heel of his boot and started walking towards Cup of Cheer. "Your mother's waiting."

Taylor threw his hands in the air and stormed after him. Why was it always impossible to talk with this man? They'd been footing around the conversation about the future of Callaway Contracting for years. And Taylor was done. He loved his job, and he loved the family company, but he wanted to know that he was fully prepared before it fell into his lap. He wanted that business degree. As he passed his truck, he opened the door, grabbed the acceptance letter, and slid it into his shirt pocket.

His father opened the coffee shop door and walked in without holding it open. Taylor snatched at the handle and stomped inside. When she saw them, his mother waved from a back corner. On the table sat 3 mugs of coffee, a plate of biscotti in front of his mother, a stack of pancakes, and a plate of eggs and bacon. His father folded himself into the chair behind the pancakes.

"Morning, Mama." Taylor leaned down and kissed his mother's cheek. She pressed her hand to his cheek, pushing their faces together for a moment before releasing him and shooing him into the chair across from her.

"Eat before it gets cold, dear. You need your protein today. You've got a big job."

With a sigh, he shoveled the eggs into his mouth in four hearty bites. The bacon, he stacked into a pile and ate all 4 four slices at once. With his mouth still full of both bacon and eggs, he chugged the entire mug of coffee and banged it down onto the table. His mother stared wide-eyed, her biscotti forgotten, and his father's fork and knife hung over his pancakes.

"Thanks for the breakfast," he said around the last remnants of food in his mouth. "Now, like I was saying-"

"Um, you've got a little something..." His mother reached across the table with a napkin and brushed at his chin, but he batted her hand away.

"Son. We brought you here for more than just your daily protein." His father cleared his throat. "We've been planning this breakfast for quite a while."

"What are you even talking about?" Taylor's eyebrows knit together in frustration.

In answer, his mother slid a white envelop across the table. He ripped into it while his eyes bounced between his parents. He pulled out a card with their company logo embossed on heavy cardstock.

"Flip it over." His mother squealed and clapped her hands.

Please join the Callaway family in celebration
As Jack retires after 37 years of service and
Taylor becomes CEO of Callaway Contacting
Drinks and Refreshments served at an Open House
December 28, 7 p.m.
Callaway Ranch

"What's this?" Taylor's voice caught in this throat.

"Oh, I knew he'd get emotional." His mother clasped his father's hand.

"Probably not for the reasons you thought of Martha." His father, Jack, slowly chewed a bite of pancake. "Why don't you tell your mother what you told me outside."

Taylor took the SMU letter out of his pocket and slid it across the table, then told her the same things he'd told his father outside.

"Oh dear." She set the letter down and looked at his father. "Well, that changes things, doesn't it?"

"I applied years ago. You guys know, SMU was my dream out of high school."

"That was a lot of years ago." His father continued to slowly eat through his pancakes.

"Ten years. Ten years, Dad." Taylor pushed back from the table, his temper rising. "I went to my reunion this past summer, and you know the first thing everyone asked me? 'You still working for your dad?' Because apparently that's all my life is meant to be."

"Nothing wrong with that. That's been the life of all Callaway's for generations."

He could hear the hurt in his father's voice. He took a deep breath and looked at his parents, really looked at them. The years had been kind to his mother as she still looked like women half her age, but years of hard labor in all varieties of weather hadn't been so kind to his father. His broad shoulders, that Taylor had inherited, were stooped as he sat at the table.

"I'm not saying there's anything wrong with that." Taylor sighed and scooted back up to the table. "I love this company, and I'm honored that you think I'm ready to take it over. But I want to know for sure I'm ready. I want to have the knowledge to take this company into an ever-changing, growing market. Now, I could get a half-assed, sorry Mama...shoddy degree from some online school and slave away my evenings and weekends for years. Or I can follow my dream, go to SMU, and do it right."

"Honey, I mean, of course we want to encourage you and support your dreams. It's just, your Daddy isn't getting any younger. And..."

"And what, Mama?"

"Well, I already mailed out all the invitations." She winced. "Which is such a silly thing to worry about, I know."

"It's not silly. You've obviously been planning this a long time." Taylor flipped the card over in his hands. "You went all the way into Gatlinburg for these, didn't you?"

"I felt awful doing it, but can you imagine the gossip if we had them made here? Everyone would have known before the day was out, and it wouldn't have been a surprise."

"Well, I can't leave you guys in a lurch. Dad, I know if you're finally admitting you're ready to retire, then it's long overdue."

"What are you trying to say, son?"

Taylor reached across the table and grabbed the SMU letter. Without a single glance at it, he crumbled it into a ball.

"I'm saying I accept." He stood and held out his hand to his father.

"Taylor, I don't know if I can let you do that." His father shook his head and laid down his silverware.

"Just let me take the gift, old man."

A smile spread on his father's face, and he finally stood to shake Taylor's hand. He grasped it and pulled him in for a back slapping hug.

"Alright, I need to get back out there. Bertha will be here any minute." Taylor took one last look at the crumpled acceptance letter and turned to head out.

Just as he set foot outside, the screech and woosh of a semi's brakes sounded down the street. Taylor tossed the retirement invitation onto the front seat of his truck and slammed the door shut. He pressed his forehead to the window, needing the cold to seep in and cool him down. It felt odd to feel so hot when he felt like a fire inside him had just been gutted, extinguished. The cold was what he needed to numb the edginess, to get him through the day. The week. The years.

With a deep breath, he pushed away from the truck. The thought of his parents seeing him so upset about such a generous gift would kill him. Besides, he had a job to do. He grabbed the drill and bit out of the back end and took off down the road.

"Big Bertha," he said quietly to himself when he reached the truck.

The scent of pine was almost overwhelming this close. Fresh cut and bound with many, many straps, Bertha lay on the semi bed held up on wooden braces. Her branches were pulled up, snug against her trunk and tied in place with rope. His whole crew had gathered around, awaiting instruction. Taylor cleared his throat but stared at the tree instead of his men. Until he reined in his thoughts, he couldn't risk the guys seeing the war of emotion he knew was showing on his face.

"Let's get the crane over here and get to work."

Taylor waved to the driver and climbed up onto the end of the trailer. Bertha's trunk was massive, easily four feet in diameter. After pulling on a pair of gloves, he rubbed his hand across the trunk's end. So many rings. So many years.

"We're going to make you shine," he said, giving the trunk a pat.

Kenny hopped up with the drill and long auger bit. Taylor marked the center of the trunk, and they took turns drilling a hole, about an inch and a half wide and a foot deep. When the bit was sunk all the way into the wood, Taylor backed it out and blew away the dust.

Randy brought over a massive metal spike, as long as a man's leg. It took both Taylor and Kenny to lift it up and slide the pointed side into the hole they'd just drilled. The clang of metal bounced off the buildings in the town square, echoing back as they pounded it in with a sledgehammer. Taylor took the first few strikes, then Kenny, then each of the guys climbed up to take a crack at it, as was tradition. Taylor began to sweat in the sunlight and his flannel shirt hit the ground. Once everyone had their turn, Taylor and Kenny finished it up until about two feet of the spike was left sticking out the bottom of the trunk.

"Alright, half of you go move the scaffolding around the hole, the rest start removing these straps." Taylor bent over with his hands on his knees, winded. He wiped the sweat from his forehead with the back of his arm.

In no time, they had the crane lined up and attached to chains on each end of Bertha. The guys worked their way around the trailer, undoing strap after strap. Finally, she was free, and Randy revved up the engine. Slowly, Bertha lifted off the braces and into the air. Randy maneuvered her over the top of the semi cab and held her just off the ground above the field. Two of the guys held guide ropes tied around the trunk to keep her from spinning. A tree trunk through Cup of Cheer's front window would ensure Mindy wouldn't be so kind as to open early for them next year.

"Hold her steady, boys." Taylor patted one of the rope guides on the back as he walked past. "Everyone else, in here and get these ties."

The rest of the crew crawled in past the massive branches to reach the ropes fastening them to the trunk. Some used knives, some used trimmers, and soon the popping of the ropes sounded like chestnuts roasting over an open fire. As the ropes were cut, the branches began to fan out, groaning slightly, as if Bertha was sighing.

Taylor moved as far into the branches as he could get. The needles pulled at his sleeves, he could feel them on his skin through the thin thermal undershirt, but still, he pressed in. When he reached the trunk, he found one of the biggest branches and began slicing into the rope that bound it. Even though he knew the outer branches should be released first, he hacked into the rope over and over, needing to see that branch free.

Just like hard work has a way of warming you up, it also demands your complete attention and soon Taylor saw nothing but the thick binding of rope in front of him. It was almost like he could feel those coils holding the branch down. He swallowed, tugging at the neckband of his shirt. The knife slipped in his sweaty hand, nicking one of his fingers. The fibers from the rope embedded in the cut, stinging and rubbing, but he didn't stop. When he was down to the last two loops of rope, a hand slammed down next to his.

"Whoa there, bud." Kenny said in a low voice. "You trying to get laid out or what?"

"I know what I'm doing, Ken."

"I've been watching you for the last three minutes or so wondering when you were gonna stop hacking away at this branch. Cause *I* know that *you* know better than to start on these inside branches by yourself."

"I've got it." Taylor said through clenched teeth.

"You going to be saying that when you cut that final loop of rope and this branch snaps out? I think you'd be lyin' flat on your back side, lucky to still have all your teeth."

Taylor pulled away from the branch with a growl. He knew Ken was right. What he was doing was reckless and stupid. Yet part of him still longed to free that branch.

"What's going on with you, man?" Kenny placed a gloved hand on Taylor's shoulder. "I've never seen you like this. Is it something with SMU?"

"Nah. It's nothing. Thanks for calling me out." Taylor shook his shoulders, trying to snap himself out of it. "I appreciate it. My dentist probably does too. Doubt he'd be too thrilled to answer an emergency call to replace my two front teeth for Christmas."

"You'd be lucky if it was just your two front teeth." Kenny patted the massive branch. "I think this thing would have you looking like Ol' Toothless Tucker."

Kenny curled his lips over his teeth and gave Taylor a ridiculous grin that did look a lot like poor Ol' Toothless Tucker, and Taylor couldn't help but laugh.

"I guarantee that look will not help in finding the future Mrs. Callaway." Kenny gave him a swat. "Now, go do your walk-through, and we'll finish up down here."

Walking through the branches once they'd been cut free was Taylor's favorite part of the whole process. He felt like he was getting up close and personal with Bertha, learning all about her. The way the trunk twisted slightly to the left. That there were more branches on a certain side. Taylor worked his way through, soaking in the woodsy smell and soft swish of the needles sliding over him.

Once he'd learned all he could with his walkthrough, he left the quiet calm of the tree to check on the scaffolding. The guys had built large wooden platforms to go around the tree base. Once Bertha was firmly cinched into the metal base inside the hole, the risers would be pushed in and secured to provide more support and excellent places for decorative gifts later.

"Ken," Taylor hollered as he inspected the scaffolding. "Our tethers ready?"

"Yes, sir." He saluted from the other side of the scaffolding. "Ready and waiting."

"I think we are a go." He turned back and gave Randy the rev-it-up signal.

With all hands on deck, they applied a new chain around Bertha, just above the middle point of her trunk. Then, they removed the two chains used to lift her off the semi. As Randy lifted the new chain higher, Bertha began to slope with her trunk toward the ground. Everyone grabbed onto the guide ropes and pulled her over to the hole.

Taylor and Kenny jumped down inside. This was the trickiest and scariest part. The spike in the trunk needed to fit into the two-inch hole in the center of the floor. With a multi-thousand-pound tree floating overhead, Taylor began to push the trunk into position.

"Pull to the right. Farther. Now to the left. Perfect." Taylor hollered up to the guys as he and Kenny situated Bertha right where they needed her. "Tell Randy to lower her in about two feet."

They waited for the message to relay then the trunk slowly descended into the metal base. After shouting a few more directions for the rope guides and Randy, the metal spike was in place. All that was left, was to tighten the clamps on the base of the tree trunk. They had to crawl around beneath the lowest, and also largest, branches that sagged into the hole. Finally, all the clamps were in place. Taylor plugged an initial string of lights into the cord they'd placed in the hole earlier.

"Now we climb." Kenny smiled at Taylor, and they reached up into the branches to pull themselves free.

They only had to climb up onto one branch to make it out of the shallow hole, but Taylor stopped to stare up. The sun was fully overhead and shown through the branches. He wasn't certain, but he thought if he looked at a certain angle, he could see the sky peeking through from the top. A patch of brilliant blue in the dim interior.

He stopped to appreciate that he got to experience something very few other people did, and it made him pause. If he got to experience something like this, that so few people did, right there in Reverence Ridge, did he really need to leave? This life. This job. These people. He could make it work, right?

On that thought, he scrambled out so the guys could get the scaffolding in place. Kenny ran to the boom truck to get the tethers tightened close to the top. Taylor jumped in to help secure the scaffolding. Once it was complete, they all took a step back while Kenny officially unclamped the chain from the crane. Bertha stood in all her glory and stayed perfectly straight.

A cheer rose from the guys, as well as the crowd that had gathered on the sidewalks. A glance at his watch showed him that church was over, and folks would be flocking to the town square to watch the progress. Mayor Davenport and the decorating team would be there soon with the boxes and boxes of massive ornaments, lights, and the silver star to grace the top.

"Another job well done, son," his father said as he walked up next to him.

"Thanks." Taylor stuffed his hands in his pockets, tipping his head back to stare up at Bertha.

"I think this is my favorite one yet." His mother wrapped an arm around his waist and sighed.

"You say that every year." Taylor shook his head and wrapped an arm around her shoulders.

"Do I?"

"Yes." Taylor and his father said at the same time.

"How'd it all go?" his father asked, trying to sound nonchalant and failing miserably.

"Went just fine. Except for the part where I about knocked myself out cutting loose an inside branch by myself."

"What?" his mother squeaked and pulled away to look at him.

"Why on earth would you do that?" His father also turned to him, his hands on his hips.

"Geez. I was just joking."

"Oh, thank goodness." His mother pressed a hand to her chest. "I'm so glad that didn't actually happen."

"Well..." Taylor knew Kenny would never keep his mouth shut and his parents would find out soon or later. "It did. But Kenny stepped up to help."

"Why would you do something so stupid?" his father growled.

"Well, I know why." His mother sighed and rested her hand on his elbow. "He's upset about SMU."

"No, Mama-"

"You don't have to lie. It's ok to be upset." She patted his arm. "I mean, we can still try to figure something out. I'm just so glad Kenny was there today. I can't even think about what could have happened. Those big branches...and you with a knife...oh my goodness..."

His mother continued to talk about all the horrible things that could have happened to him, but Taylor didn't hear anything after she mentioned Kenny. He knew how lucky he was to have his best friend still working with him. They'd saved each other's butts more times than either of them could remember. And it got a thought churning in Taylor's mind.

"I have an idea." Taylor said slowly. "It just came to me, so tell me if it's too crazy."

Taylor leaned in and talked in hushed tones with his parents. If he could convince them of this plan, maybe, just maybe, everything would work out for everyone. He felt that little flame inside him flicker back to life, ignited by hope.

His mother was easy to convince. She agreed as soon as the idea was out of his mouth. His father on the other hand took some convincing, but finally he agreed with a simple nod. That was all Taylor needed, and he took off to his truck to grab the retirement invitation. Then he hurried back to his parents, who'd moved over to talk to Kenny as he came down in the bucket of the boom truck.

"Great job with those tethers, Ken." He shook his friend's hand as he climbed out.

"Phew. We got a real beaut this year. Don't you think Mrs. Callaway?"

"One of the finest I've seen yet." She smiled and leaned her head back to look up to the top of the tree. "This is Bertha number what? How many have we had now?"

"Bertha number twelve." Taylor shook his head and grinned. "We've been naming them that since we started working at sixteen."

"That has been a long time." His mom winked at Taylor and made a nodding motion towards Kenny.

"Um, yeah. It has been a long time." Taylor cleared his throat, suddenly nervous at his best friend's response. "We got a little something for you, man."

Kenny looked at Taylor suspiciously, then shrugged. Taylor handed him the invitation first. As Kenny read it, realization spread across his face.

"You're retiring, sir? No way. Congrats." He rushed in to give Jack a hug. Over his shoulder he whispered to Taylor "Did you tell them?"

"I did." Taylor nodded. He looked down and scuffed his boots in the grass. "With the old man retiring, there isn't really any way for me to go away for four years."

"Oh, man, I'm so sorry, Bro."

"Unless...." Taylor chewed on his lip but looked up at his best friend. "Unless you become a partner and don't mind running things while I'm gone."

Kenny blinked multiple times but didn't say anything for a long moment. Taylor was beginning to think he would turn them down, until his friend broke into his trademark happy dance. Hips and hands swinging in circles, he spun around with a holler.

"Are you kidding me?"

"Nope."

"Best Christmas gift ever. I don't know how to thank you guys."

"Just say you accept, and we can start on the paperwork tomorrow."

"You guys really trust me with this?"

"Kenny, you've been working this job as long as I have. There's literally no one in the world I'd trust to do this more than you."

"Well, hot dogs! Sign me up."

Kenny pulled all three of the Callaways into a group hug. He even got Mrs. Callaway to join him in the happy dance. Another thing Taylor inherited from his father was the 'I-don't-dance' gene. They both stood with their arms crossed and slight smiles on their lips as the mayor and her crew showed up with multiple trucks to unload.

"Alright you two," Taylor said, "let's go help Mayor Davenport."

They left Taylor's parents to head across the field.

"So, if we're partners, does that mean we'll add my name to the company logo?"

"I suppose so. I hadn't really thought about it yet."

"Callaway Alvarez Contracting." Kenny held his hands up as he said it. "Oh, or maybe Alvarez Callaway Contracting."

"No."

"Oh, come on. It's alphabetical order."

"Still no."

"Hold up." Kenny stopped walking. "Does this mean that my kids and my kids' kids will work for our company too? Just like you always knew you would?"

"I suppose so. If they want to."

"Right." Kenny started walking again, a satisfied grin on his face. "I'm so glad you're getting to go to SMU. I'm really happy for you."

"Thanks. It's taken a few extra years, but I guess dreams really do come true."

Macy

The plane bounced down the runway and screeched to a halt. Macy looked out the window of their tiny prop plane and let out the breath she'd been holding. She released her death grip on the armrests and Brinley grabbed her hand, bouncing in her seat. Her golden hair floated around her face, partly because of her angelic qualities, but mostly because of static.

"We're here, Mom." Brinley smiled and turned back to the window.

Macy was still getting used to the new name. Mom. It made her heart flutter every time she heard it, and she wondered if that would ever go away. She hoped it wouldn't.

Brinley had been in foster care since the age of six. She'd lived with Macy for the past year, but before adoption was an option, Macy insisted on being called by her first name. She'd had too many kids come and go to be certain of anything, but several months back, word came through and the adoption was finally official, just in time for Christmas.

"Come on, Sweet Girl. Let's get off this plane and see what there is to see."

Macy helped Brinley into her coat and then shrugged on her own. She grabbed their carry-on bags and ushered Brinley in front of her down the aisle. A set of stairs had been pushed up to the plane door for them to walk down, and it led them outside.

"I have never been on such a tiny plane or been to such a small airport in my life," Macy muttered, and pulled her coat firmly around her neck.

"Isn't it just perfect?" Brinley glanced back at her as she stepped off the stairs. "It's like it's just for us."

They walked across the tarmac, into the airport, and through the single gate towards security and baggage claim. Besides themselves and the handful of others on their flight, the airport was all but deserted.

Macy wrung her hands together as they waited for their suitcases. Maybe coming to this small of a town was a mistake. She'd never even heard of Reverence Ridge, Tennessee until a few days ago when they were trying to decide where to go for a celebratory Christmas trip. Macy had suggested New York City with Rockefeller Center, or the Florida Keys for a beach holiday. But in a single article listing Christmas destinations, Reverence Ridge popped up, and Brinley was instantly smitten. She wouldn't even consider other more exciting or grand locales.

"There they are." Brinley stretched up to see their bags. "I'll get them."

With suitcases in tow, they made their way to the car rental counter. The single employee perked up as they approached.

"Good morning, friends. Do you have a reservation?"

"Yes, under Macy Doyle."

"And Brinley Doyle."

Brinley had her mittened fingers gripped onto the counter edge as she beamed up at Macy. She'd been saying her full name, new last name included, whenever possible since the adoption. Macy threw an arm around Brinley's shoulders and pulled her in for a hug.

"Wonderful. And I have you returning on the twenty-sixth, is that correct?"

"Um. Just a moment." She knelt in front of Brinley and whispered, "It's not too late. We could still drive over to Gatlinburg and Pigeon Forge to do the Christmas celebration at Dollywood. Or head down to Atlanta or Savannah. Somewhere a little more exciting?"

"Nope." Brinley didn't hesitate before shaking her head. "Reverence Ridge."

"Ok." Macy sighed. "We have eight days, so we could always do day trips or overnights if we run out of things to do here."

"Oh, you'll have a fantastic time in Reverence Ridge," the car rental employee said. "Our Christmas festivities are the best, the real star at the top of the Christmas tree, if you will."

"See, Mom? Someone who lives here would know." Brinley gave her that 'duh' look that pre-teens are so fond of. "We definitely want the star on the tree for our first Christmas as a family, don't we?"

"Laying it on a little thick there, huh? Yes, of course, that's what we want." Macy turned back to the counter. "So, yes, we'll be returning on the twenty-sixth."

"Wonderful. I've got you in our last Ho-Ho-Honda." The employee passed her the keys and waved as they headed out the door.

"I thought it would be warmer here." Brinley shivered and flipped her hood up.

"Me too. Let's hurry." Macy pushed the button on the keys, and they headed toward their car.

They tossed their suitcases into the trunk of the red sedan and hurried to the doors. Inside, Macy plugged the address of their B&B into her GPS. It was just a few miles down the highway, a quick drive after a long flight. Looking around at the nothingness outside the airport, Macy prayed their cell service would hold out.

"I don't know about you, but I could use a good leg stretch and something warm to eat." Macy moved the seat back to sit straight and placed her hands at ten and two on the wheel.

"Oh, yeah." Brinley agreed. "Some eggs and pancakes. Or maybe a BLT. Is it breakfast or lunch time?"

"This is the magical time of brunch, where you may eat whatever your heart desires. Maybe pancakes and a BLT? Or Spaghetti and meatballs with a waffle on the side?"

"You're silly, Mom," Brinley giggled and then turned to stare out the window as they pulled onto the highway.

The road was narrow and winding. Tall trees pressed in on one side with a field and a view of mountains on the other, nothing like the dry, sandy desert back in Phoenix. Brinley's nose was pressed to the glass, fogging it up with each breath. Macy shook her head and smiled.

"Wow. This is like a total winter wonderland." Brinley wiggled in her seat,enthralled with the scenery.

Snow dusted the ground and the gray clouds above made Macy think more could be coming before the day was over. The thought of driving through snow made her nervous, and she straightened even more in her seat. Record high temps she could deal with. Frozen stuff on the road, she could not.

"Have you seen snow before, Brin?"

"Nope. I read that the last time Phoenix had snow was in 1998. That was *way* before I was born."

"Oh, here's the sign for Reverence Ridge." Macy pointed out the windshield.

Next to the road was a brightly painted wooden sign. In scrolling red font, it read 'Reverence Ridge. Where Christmas is Revered.' Underneath the words was a painting of an idyllic small town decorated to the hilt for Christmas and covered in a perfect layer of white snow.

"What does 'revered' mean?" Brinley sounded out the word.

"It means respected and admired."

"Well, I've got to revere a town that reveres Christmas that much." Brinley giggled. "Can you imagine living in a Christmas town all year round?"

"No. No, I cannot." Macy shook her head. "I think it would lose a little of its magic if I had to live it every day."

"Not me." Brinley said sternly. "I don't think I could ever get tired of Christmas."

Macy's heart twinged. Brinley never went into much detail about her life before foster care, but from the bits she'd mentioned, Macy had the feeling she'd never gotten a real Christmas celebration before.

Macy couldn't even imagine. Her childhood had been filled with over the top celebrations, especially at Christmas. It was still a yearly tradition for her and her sister to try and outdo each other this time of year. Who could get their parents the best gift? Who could make the biggest gingerbread house? Who could throw the most extravagant Christmas party? Honestly, by the time January rolled around, Macy was glad it would be a whole year until Christmas came around again. It was exhausting.

They came over the crest of a hill, and in front of them, Reverence Ridge sat nestled in a valley surrounded by rocky, tree-covered slopes.

Macy slowed the car to a crawl as they entered Main Street. Brinley was silent as they passed houses decorated with boughs of fresh pine and red ribbons. The trees in the front yards were decorated with strands of beads, lights, and popcorn.

Macy's heart sank when they turned at the town square. They'd already made it halfway through Reverence Ridge? It'd only been a few blocks. How could there possibly be enough to do for over a week in such a small place?

They stopped in front of a sign for The Night Before Bed and Breakfast. The house looked like it should be out in the forest, with its dark wooden siding and green tin roof. But it seemed to fit right here in the center of town, too. Macy parked on the street, and they wheeled their suitcases up the front walk. Brinley was practically vibrating with excitement.

They both shook off the cold when they walked into the foyer. Deep red wallpaper decorated in a golden floral made the small space feel warm even as a cold gust followed them inside. Dark wooden furniture and the aroma of baking cookies added to that cozy feeling.

"Hello. Hello." A short, plump woman pushed through a swinging door, wiping her hands on her apron. Her graying hair was piled high on her head and her cheeks were bright and rosy. "You must be Macy. And you must be Brinley. Welcome to The Night Before."

"Thank you, Miss..." Macy reached out a hand.

"Oh, honey, you just call me Harriet." She clasped Macy's hands and gave it a hearty shake. "We're all on a first name basis around here."

"Miss. Harriet, this is our first Christmas as a family." Brinley gushed. "I was just adopted, so we wanted to go on a special trip to celebrate."

"Well now, this is an extra special time for you two."

"It sure is." Macy smiled. "Do you know what room we're in? I don't want to keep you."

"Oh, pish," Harriet waved a hand at them. "I'm just getting some things together formlunch. Nothing that won't hold for a few minutes. Why don't I show you to your room? I'm sure you'd like to get unpacked and settled."

"That sounds lovely. Thank you, Harriet."

"My pleasure, darling. It's what I'm here for." Harriet walked them over to a staircase and started up.

As Brinley told Harriet all about their plane ride, Macy took in more of the B&B. All the wood was polished to a shine. Each nook and corner held a seating area, so even though the living space wasn't massive, it could easily hold quite a few people. And each little seating area had its own decoration style, like Harriet couldn't decide on just one and went with them all. One had a nativity. One was all snowmen. One was all reindeer. Macy's logic said it shouldn't work, but it came together like something you'd find on a Pinterest board.

Upstairs, they turned to the left and stopped next to the banister as Harriet pulled an old metal key from her apron pocket. She opened their door and then slid the key into Macy's hand.

"I know they're old school and a little cumbersome, but I just love the feel of the lock tumblers clicking, and you just can't get that with any of the newer key options."

"I imagine not." Macy slid the key into her purse pocket for safe-keeping.

"If you need anything at all, dears, I'm right downstairs."

With that, she shuffled down the hallway, and they pushed into their room. Macy had expected an abundance of lace and floral, but they walked into another room that could easily grace the cover of a magazine. A four-post bed with plush navy sheets sat in the center of the room. The walls were a tonal gray wallpaper in a pine branch design. The accenting curtains and pillows were a sumptuous wine color. Garlands hung around the dresser mirror and electric candles sat in the bay window.

"Mom! Mom! Come look."

Macy glanced around the room and didn't see Brinley until she popped her head around a corner on the other side of the bed.

"Well, I'll be," Macy declared as she walked around to found a little nook that had been outfitted with a twin bed and a dresser.

Next to the dresser was a small table covered with a Christmas village, but the houses were all open on the front so you could see inside the rooms like a dollhouse. Brinley sat next to it moving the people from one house to another.

"This place is amazing," she said softly.

"Wouldn't this be the perfect place for all your Barbies?" Macy crouched next to Brinley to get a better look.

There were seven buildings in all. A bakery, post office, church, and several houses. All of them had perfectly sized furniture and all the decorations. They were nothing like the new dollhouses with moving elevators and fountains, but Macy had to admire the craftsmanship.

She wondered if a few dolls and houses really compared to the shows and rides at Dollywood. Or church choirs, window shopping, and the tree lighting in New York City. She hoped they hadn't made a mistake coming here.

"Well, how about we take a few minutes to get unpacked, and then we go get something to eat and figure out what there is to do around here?"

"Ok." Brinley looked up at her with a smile.

Macy returned to her part of the room and laid out her suitcase. Soon, all her clothes were folded in the dresser or hung in the closet.

With a sigh, she sat on the edge of the bed and pulled out her phone. Before she could open the browser to find the calendar of events, it began to ring. Macy looked at the name on the screen and groaned inwardly.

"Hey, Mags." Macy plastered a fake smile on her face even though her sister couldn't actually see her.

"Macy .Hey girl. How are you? Did you get in ok?"

"Hey, yeah. We're fine. Just getting settled in our room."

"Oh, in that B&B. Is it awful? How bad is it?"

"Actually," Macy looked around again, "It's really nice. Feels very warm and cozy."

"Ah. Cozy. I figured something in that town would be pretty small."

"The B&B is actually quite large. And our room turned out to be a suite." Macy knew full well the nook didn't classify as a suite, but the need to embellish the truth a little came out whenever Mags was involved. "Brin has her own room to sleep in that's decorated with this beautiful village of doll houses."

"That is just precious, Macy. Pre-cious. So, are you gals getting dolled up to head out on the town tonight?"

"Probably not. It's a lot colder than I expected." Macy thought through the clothes she'd packed. "We'll probably just wear whatever's warmest today and see what the forecast is for the rest of the week."

"Oh, you little Vixen, you." Maggie laughed. "Well, hey, girl, I gotta jet. Like literally. We decided on a last-minute trip to Aspen since you won't be around for our usual soiree. Just wouldn't be the same without family."

"What about mom and dad?"

"Oh, they're coming with us. So don't you worry about them. We've got everything taken care of. You just enjoy your time in...where are you again?"

"Tennessee. Smoky Mountains." Macy hung her head and rubbed her temple with her free hand.

"That's right. The gool ol' Smokies. Not quite like the Rockies. More like tall hills, right?"

"Alright, Mags. Hope you all have a fantastic time. We'll catch up when we all get back home."

"Ok, girl. You give Brin a big hug from Auntie Maggie."

"Will do."

Macy flopped back onto the bed with a growl. Last year, she'd have jumped on the first plane to Aspen to surprise them all. This year, while that option still sounded tempting, she had Brinley to think about.

She pulled out her phone again to get back to the task of finding the schedule of events. A quick search showed a couple activities in neighboring cities, but nothing in Reverence Ridge. Even the town's website had no schedule of events anywhere. She quickly made note of the activities close by and called Brinley to go.

"I'm not finding anything for events online," Macy said as the walked downstairs, her fingers still scrolling on the phone screen.

"Why don't we just ask Miss Harriet? I'm sure she'll know everything there is to do here."

"Good idea. I'm sure there must be a website I'm missing or something."

They could hear Harriet in the kitchen, so they pushed through the swinging door. She stood on the other side of a massive butcher block island rolling out sugar cookie dough and swaying to Nat King

Cole. She hummed slightly off tune as Macy sighed at the warm smell of vanilla and sugar.

"All settled in?" Harriet greeted them with a smile.

"Yes, that little nook for Brinley is just perfect."

"As soon as I heard you were bringing a young lady, I knew that room was for you. Did you find my doll houses?"

"I did. They are so beautiful." Brinley began to twirl to the song, too. "I've never seen anything like them."

"I'd expect not. My Papa made them for me when I was a girl."

"So cool."

"We're sorry to interrupt your baking, but we were wondering if you could suggest somewhere to get some brunch." Macy asked. "And if you know of a website where all the local activities and events are listed."

"Oh, you'll want to look at the Nice List for that." Harriet went back to rolling out her cookie dough. "Walk to the end of the block, and on each corner of the town square there's a lamp post with the Nice List attached. That will tell you all the nice things to do around town for the day."

"A lamp post? There isn't just a website I could look at?" Macy pointed to her phone.

"Humph." Harriet snorted. "This town has used the Nice List for longer than the internet has existed. They do just fine."

"Um, ok then." Macy blinked slowly, astonished. "How about food?"

"Well, you've got two options for that." Harriet gently pressed copper cutters into the dough and slid the cookies onto a baking sheet. "We've got Cup of Cheer right on the square for coffee, sandwiches, soups, and such. If you want something warmer, the diner, Wonderful

Thyme, is on the other end of the square. The roast beast and hash is to die for."

"Thank you." Macy slid an arm around Brinley's shoulder and turned her towards the door. "Let's go, Brin. I'm starved."

"Bundle up, girls. It's supposed to be a cold one today." Harriet called out as the swinging door shut behind them. "Don't forget the Nice List. Maybe check it twice."

They stopped at the door so Brinley could tug on her pink hat with the glittery pompom and matching mittens. She zipped her coat up to her chin and wrapped a scarf around her neck before they opened the door to head out. A cold wind hit them as soon as they were beyond the protection of the porch. Small flakes flurried around them, dancing in the air.

"Man, I'm wishing I grabbed a hat right about now. My ears are going to freeze." Macy reached up to cover them. Her short hair offered no protection from the cold air. "I'm thinking something warm sounds good. What about you?"

"Definitely."

They ducked their heads and walked quickly down the sidewalk. Less than a block down, they arrived at the town square. After a brief, teeth chattering conversation,they decided to hurry to the diner and look at all the square had to offer once they were warmed up.

Wonderful Thyme sat at the far end. It's white brick façade with brown awnings looked cozy next to all the other stucco shops surrounding it. Inside, they were shown right to a booth at the front of the restaurant, with a window view. Brinley kicked her legs under the table as they looked at the menu.

"Have you decided?" an older gentleman came to their table and asked.

"The Roast Beast and hash came highly recommended, so I think I'll go with that." Macy folded her menu and handed it to the server.

"I want the Polar Excess." Brinley's eyes were huge as she smiled at the server.

"Oh, are you sure?" The man laughed. "I don't know if someone as small as you can eat all that."

Brinley looked through her lashes at Macy, questioningly. Macy gave her a small nod, and Brinley's smile returned.

"I'm sure."

Pretty soon their food arrived. Brinley slowly worked her way through three big plates. One of peppermint pancakes, one of eggs and bacon, and one of cheesy grits and a biscuit. Harriet had been right; Macy's roast and hash were delicious. She finished her food and sat back to scroll through her phone and look for more activities in the area. She was certain it had to be listed somewhere online, but, by the time Brinley finished her food, she'd still found nothing. They shared a figgy pudding, which neither had tried before and both decided they could do without trying again.

"Let's go check out the Nice List." Macy sighed as they shrugged on their coats. "Someone needs to bring this town into the twenty-first century. They're missing out on so much publicity and visibility."

"Mom. You said no work talk this week," Brinley pouted. "You promised."

"You're right, Sweet Girl. I'm sorry."

It was early afternoon when they left the crowded diner, but it seemed like evening with how dark it had become. The wind was blowing high above them in the trees, but the shops on all sides kept them pretty protected in the square. They hurried across the street to the corner to one of the lampposts. Flame flickered in the glass globe at the top. Attached to the side of the post was a clear box lined with red velvet. Hanging from the box was an intricately carved wooden sign. Macy marveled for a moment at the detailed swirl of elves, ribbons, and paper painted in reds and greens that formed the words Nice List.

"How about we head back to the B&B and make a plan of action?" Macy took a quick picture of the list inside the box before stuffing her phone and hand back into her pocket. "Then we won't be wandering aimlessly out in the cold."

"Can't we just see what's around here? Look at all these cute shops," Brinley said through chattering teeth, "and we have to see the tree."

"Baby, you're shivering. Let's get warmed up. Maybe put on another layer and decide what we want to do." Macy rubbed up and down Brin's arms in an attempt to warm her up. "We'll be here all week and have plenty of time to see everything."

"Fine." Brinley kicked at the dusting of snow on the ground.

As they trudged back, Macy's concerns grew. She pulled out her phone and zoomed in on the picture of the activities list and hoped there were more options on it than she imagined. Once they got back to the B&B, she could read it and write out a schedule for them. Then they wouldn't miss anything.

Brinley stopped and pressed her face up to every window they walked past. She wanted to see the bookstore. She begged to walk through the general store. She pouted as they hurried past the Christmas tree. By the time they reached the end of the square, Macy was practically tugging her down the street.

When they got back to The Night Before, Brinley yanked her arm free of Macy's hand and ran up the front walk. As Macy made it through the front door, she could hear Brinley thudded up the stairs. Macy closed her eyes for a moment before heading up.

When she reached the top of the stairs, Brinley was leaning against the wall next to their door. Her arms were crossed, and she was staring at her shoes like they were the most fascinating things in the universe. Macy pulled the heavy golden key from her purse with a sigh and opened the door. Before she could say anything, Brinley rushed in and disappeared into her bedroom nook.

Macy sat on the bench at the end of the bed to slip off her boots. As she rubbed some warmth back into her feet, she looked around again. All the warm wooden furniture in the room made her feel like she could have been inside a gingerbread house, which lifted her spirits and made her smile. The dresser and the bench she sat on were simplistic, but with care taken in the details. She ran her finger down the edge of the bench, feeling the glossy wood for herself. Small flourishes of carving added a hint of detail to the corners and reminded her of the Nice List sign.

A very talented carpenter must call Reverence Ridge home, she thought.

She had to fight the urge to slip into work mode, imagining several online marketing plans to showcase such talent. Shaking her head, she pushed off the bench and rolled her shoulders. The early morning trip to the airport was starting to get to her. And if it was getting to her, it had to be getting to Brinley.

Macy peeked around the corner into the small bedroom nook. Brinley was curled up on the bed, her golden hair spilling onto the pillow from underneath her hat. Macy quietly picked the coat up off the floor and knelt next to the bed. She slid off Brinley's boots and gently lifted her head to pull off the hat. Brinley's eyelashes fluttered on her cheek, but she didn't wake up. Macy pulled up the blanket and tucked it around her.

"A little rest does sound nice," Macy said to herself as she climbed into her own bed. "Let's just look at the events schedule and make a plan first."

The bed felt like a dream. She pulled the comforter up under her chin, sinking into the cloud of warmth. It seeped up through her toes, her legs, her back. As she zoomed in on the picture of the events schedule again, each part of her relaxed into the comfort.

Macy opened her eyes. She hadn't even realized they'd slid closed. The room was dark, and when she glanced down at her phone, she saw that two hours had passed. It was still quiet in Brinley's nook, so Macy stretched out and made a plan for the evening. In the next town over, there was a nice restaurant with good online reviews. After talking to Maggie, the idea of getting dressed up and having a fancy dinner with her daughter sent a shiver of excitement through her. She could even have the waiter take their picture so she could send it to her sister later.

"Brinley," she called out as she slipped out from under the covers. "Time to get up sleepyhead."

She found herself humming as she ran a comb through her hair and planned what to wear for the evening. Tilting her head to hear, only silence came from Brinley's nook.

"Brin, come on," she called from the seat at the dresser mirror. "I have a fun plan for a fancy dinner tonight. We can get all dressed up. Brin?"

Macy walked over to the nook and flipped the light switch. The little village came to life with blinking Christmas lights, but Brinley was nowhere to be seen. Cold terror gripped Macy's heart.

"Brinley?" Macy tore the blankets off the bed. "Brinley, this isn't funny."

Her breath came in sharp gasps as she spun in a circle, looking for any clue. A foot sticking out from under the bed. A half-closed closet door. A bulging curtain. But there was nothing. Everything looked as it should.

She ran to the door and yanked it open, but more silence greeted her. No sounds filtered up from the kitchen. No voices from the sitting room. Macy turned back and slammed her feet into her boots, then took off down the stairs.

"Brinley? Brinley?"

More silence.

Macy slammed open the kitchen door, her heart moving similarly against her ribcage. But the room was dark and cold. She raced back up the stairs hoping to find some sitting area she hadn't known about where Brinley was reading a book or watching tv. She ran to the end of the hall, finding only locked doors. Fear like she'd never felt before tore at her chest.

"Brinley? Baby, I'm sorry for earlier. Please come out."

Macy hollered her name over and over as she returned to their room, throwing open closet doors and turning on all the lights. But Brinley was nowhere to be found and there was only one place left to look. Outside.

Macy grabbed her coat as she ran out the door and thundered down the stairs. She had one arm in the sleeve when she flew out the door, looking both directions down the street. Where would she go? Where would she go? Macy only had to think a moment before turning towards the town square.

If only she'd taken more time that afternoon. If only she hadn't been in such a rush to get back to the B&B. Her thoughts spiraled back to earlier as she jogged down the street. Her breath came out in hard, fast puffs. She peeked down the side of every house she passed. As she turned to look down a side yard, she bumped into someone.

"Macy, dear. What are you doing over here?" Harriet caught onto both her arms to steady them both.

"Brinley. She's gone." Macy could hardly push the words out between the emotion and lack of oxygen. "I...I can't find her."

"I just saw her." Harriet's words were rushed as she turned to point behind her toward the square. "Just there, by the tree. Go. Go."

Macy was off running before she finished speaking. Why hadn't she listened? Why couldn't she just give Brinley the Christmas that she wanted? That she deserved? Why'd she have to try turning it into something else? Why...Why?

The tree stood in front of her, shining white light across the field. Booths that hadn't been there earlier were set up along the perimeter and people filled the whole square, walking from stall to stall and sitting at folding tables. She crossed the street, narrowly missing being trampled by a horse-drawn carriage. She heard yelling behind her but didn't stop to look.

By the tree, Harriet had said. Macy looked all around but didn't see Brinley. Macy's eyes darted from face to face. She rounded the back side of the Christmas tree and finally spotted a pink, glittery hat. She clutched her chest and hurried over to where Brinley sat on a bench, staring up at the tree.

"Brinley," Macy collapsed to her knees in front of her daughter. "Brinley. Oh, thank God you're ok."

She pulled her in to a fierce hug until her heart stopped hammering and she could breathe again. Brinley sat frozen for a moment and then wrapped her arms around Macy's neck.

"Mom, what are you doing here?" Brinley said with her face pressed into Macy's shoulder.

"What am *I* doing here?" Macy sputtered and pulled Brinley to face her. "What are *you* doing here? You scared me half to death."

"You seemed so stressed earlier, I didn't want to wake you up." Brinley's eyes dropped to the ground. "I just stopped to look for a minute and was on my way back. I promise."

"Listen, Brin," Macy pulled herself up onto the bench next to her and leaned in so their faces were close. "I know you were mad at me earlier, but you can't run off like this. It isn't safe."

"I wasn't running off." Brinley's eyebrows creased in confusion.

"Well, then what are you doing out here and not safe and warm in our room?"

"Getting your Christmas present." Brinley placed a small gift bag in Macy's lap.

"Getting my what?"

"Your present." Brinley shrugged. "I was going to give it to you tonight anyway, so you may as well open it."

Macy brushed the tips of her fingers against the tan bag in her lap. The look in Brinley's eyes erased any remaining fear and anger as Macy pulled out the dark brown tissue paper. She pulled it aside and smiled at what lay there. A fur-lined pink hat with earflaps and white tassels.

"I thought you'd like this kind to keep your ears warm." Brinley picked it up and held out the ear flaps. "And so we can match. I've always wanted something to match my mom."

Brinley's voice dropped so low for the last few words that Macy could hardly hear them. But their lack of volume didn't diminish their heavy weight. Tears prickled the corners of Macy's eyes, and she pulled Brinley into another hug.

"I absolutely love it." Macy rested her head on the glittery pom pom of Brinley's hat. "It's the most thoughtful and beautiful gift anyone's ever given me."

"Really?" Brinley squeaked.

"Definitely." Macy sat back with a giant grin. She slid the hat onto her head and twirled the tassels. "How do I look?"

"Beautiful."

"Just like you, Sweet Girl." Macy booped her nose.

"Can we get a picture?" Brinley lit up. "In front of the tree?"

They both stood and Macy took roughly fifty selfies of them in front of the massive tree. When they both exhausted their model pose knowledge, they sat back on the bench. They leaned back and stared at the tree in silence for a few minutes. Giant blue, purple, and green ornaments hung on the branches, lit by twinkling white lights. The star at the top glistened like it was made of ice crystals.

"You really thought I ran away?" Brinley asked suddenly.

"I knew you were upset with me earlier." Macy said apologetically. "I feel like I owe you an apology."

"No, I understand."

"You do?"

"Yeah. You wanted to have a big, fancy Christmas together."

"You're right. I did." Macy nodded and took a deep breath. "But not anymore."

"What do you mean?"

"The way I was raised, you showed someone how much you loved them by how much you spent on their gift. My sister and I always try to outdo each other with big gifts and crazy parties." Macy stopped and grabbed Brinley's mittened hand. "But today, when I was running around looking for you…this may sound cheesy, but I realized that none of that mattered."

"You did?"

"What mattered was spending time with you. My daughter. Isn't that what this whole trip was about? Being a family?"

"Being a family." Brinley beamed.

"So, from now on, no more schedules and plans. Let's just do what we feel like when we feel like it."

"Seriously?" Brinley raised an eyebrow. "No plans?"

"Ok, well I can't promise we won't plan anything. But I'll stop trying to turn this trip into something big and crazy. We'll just enjoy everything Reverence Ridge has to offer."

"I like that plan." Brinley giggled and then her tummy rumbled loud enough for them both to hear.

"Well, ok then. I know what we need to do next. I made this idea to get all dressed up and drive over to a nice restaurant, but something around here smells amazing."

They both sniffed the air and nodded. Following their noses, they arrived at a booth selling giant bowls of spicy corn chowder and biscuits. After the soup, they found another vendor selling cups of hot chocolate and cookies. Each with a steaming cup in one hand and a cookie in the other, they started a lap around the square to look at all the decorations.

"Brin," Macy said. "Promise me you'll never go off on your own like that again, please."

"I promise, Mom." Brinley slid her arm through Macy's. "I won't do it again."

"Thank you."

"I just wanted to get you a nice gift. To thank you for everything you've done for me."

"Oh, Brin. You don't have to thank me. Being your mom is the greatest gift I could have ever hoped for."

Everleigh

E verleigh brushed a final layer of glitter across her eyelids and stood back to admire her reflection. It was a special day, so she'd busted out all her favorites. Her dusky eyeshadow, with its layer of silver glitter, contrasted nicely with her cherry red lipstick. Her eyebrows were plucked and filled to perfection, both cheek bones popped with a gold bronzer, and her nose was contoured to adorableness.

Everleigh grabbed her phone and pressed the volume to the max. As Chuck Berry's wicked guitar riffs and upbeat lyrics blasted from the small speaker, she bopped from her bathroom to the bedroom. The outfit she picked out last night waited for her on the sunny paisley chair next to her bed. As Chuck encouraged Rudolph to run, run, Everleigh pulled on her warmest pair of long underwear. Not the most fashionable, but necessary in her line of work. Over those she pulled on a pair of flowy black pants and an extra chunky red sweater.

She squealed a little when she slid the necklace of golden sleigh bells over her head and large wreath earrings into each ear. To complete the look, she tied each braided pigtail with red tinsel garland. Her heavy-duty black boots waited next to the front door, ready to get her through one of the busiest mail delivery days of the year. Before opening the door, she paused for a moment, wondering if there was any way to make her look more festive. Then she remembered her elf shoe boot covers.

"You're slippin', girl." She shook her head and grabbed the boot covers, purse, and a special gift she'd spent far too long wrapping.Before walking outside into the silent, early morning, she paused her phone in the middle of one of T. Swifts upbeat holiday tunes.

It was still dark enough to see the stars from her small porch, but just the hint of sunrise was showing over the mountaintops. The air was cold, crisp, and invigorating. At least it felt dry, and it hadn't snowed overnight, so there was no need to scrape the windshield. She pulled at the door of her well-loved Fiesta. The groans as it begrudgingly inched open felt obscenely loud in the still morning. Cringing, she thought for the hundredth time that picking a car based solely on its name wasn't the best philosophy. But shouldn't a car called Fiesta be a lot more fun than this poor rust bucket? It was irony at its finest.

As soon as she was inside and the engine finally agreed to turn over, the radio clicked on to the local morning show. Her heart pattered a little faster as a deep, sultry voice filled her car.

"We have a local time of 6:10 on this lovely Tuesday morning. Current temps at about thirty-eight. So, bundle up folks it's a chilly one. It should be nice and sunny until later tonight when we have a chance of snow. Stay tuned after these messages for our favorite part of the morning show, *Everleigh tells Everything*."

As she pulled out of her driveway and creeped down the road, she had her phone at the ready. She chewed her lip, waiting impatiently for it to ring. Even though she was expecting it, she still jumped slightly when her phone chirped. She answered it on speaker, the phone resting in her lap as she kept both hands on the wheel.

"Good morning, Buck."

"How's my favorite lady this morning?"

"I'm great," she responded. "How are you?"

"Better now that you're on the line."

"Oh, Buck." She could feel her cheeks heating up as she rounded the corner onto Main Street. Today had to be the day he finally asked her out. It just had to be. They'd been having these morning calls every weekday for months.

"Alright, our commercial is up in ten, hold on."

The line went silent briefly as he clicked back on air. Everleigh tapped her fingers on the wheel and glanced around at the dark houses. Soon, the lights would come on and the town would be bustling with holiday shoppers and tourists, but right now it was just hers.

"We're back on the air with Everleigh, our favorite morning know-it-all." Buck's voice felt overly loud after the silence.

"Correction, Buck." Everleigh pulled the phone up to her ear. "I tell it all. I would never claim to know it all."

"Pardon me, folks. I stand corrected." Papers rustled in the background. "We had someone write in a question for you, Ev."

"Really?" She wasn't surprised. People always wanted to know something. "Do tell."

"Dear Ms. Tells Everything," Buck began to read. "Oh, very formal."

"I like it. Continue."

"I don't know what to get my girlfriend for Christmas this year. We've been together long enough that it needs to be something nice, but not long enough that it needs to be something extra nice, if you catch my drift. Help. Signed Clueless at Christmas."

"Well, Clueless, thanks for the abundance of details." Everleigh sighed and shook her head. "But seriously, gift giving is itself kind of a gift. Did you know, Buck, that gifts are actually one of the five love languages?"

"Um. Love languages? No. I can confidently say that I did not know that."

"Yeah, so, for some people giving gifts is the way they show love. For some people, the way they want to be shown love is by receiving gifts. So, if Clueless's girlfriend is the type who's love language is receiving gifts, he'll really need to put some thought into it."

"Come on, seriously? There are so many better ways to show love than buying people stuff. That's just materialistic."

"Well, Buck, you obviously have a different love language. But don't scoff at other people's preferred way of showing or receiving love.'

"Ok. Ok. Sorry folks. I'm still learning here." Buck chuckled. "So, Ev, what's your love language?"

"Well, very fitting for this conversation, my main way of expressing love is through gifts. I put a lot of thought into a present, probably too much time actually. I always remember little things people say about what they need or want."

"And what about receiving love?"

"Well, wouldn't you like to know." Everleigh smiled slyly as she pulled into a parking spot. "Back to Clueless's question. Gifts should be heartfelt, not necessarily expensive. If you want to make your girlfriend happy, listen and watch for things that she needs or that could make her life easier. Does she have hobbies? Are there any pampering products that she won't buy for herself but you just know she'd enjoy? With a little thought, anyone can give an amazing gift."

"Spoken like a true expert."

"Well, I myself have a special gift to deliver today." She looked down at the pristinely wrapped gift in the passenger seat. "So, I am speaking from very recent experience."

"Oh, and who is the lucky recipient of this gift?"

"That is top secret, Buck."

"Is it for someone I know?"

"We live in Reverence Ridge. Everyone knows everyone here."

"So, that's a yes." Buck sounded triumphant. "Well, there you have it, folks. *Everleigh Tells Everything*. Hope you learned a little something. I know I did. Until tomorrow, Ev."

"Thanks, Buck. Happy Monday, Ridgers."

Everleigh sat in her car as the line went silent. She waited for a few moments, staring out at the coffeeshop in front of her. Its lights shown onto the dark street, welcoming her, beckoning her to come indulge in an over-caffeinated beverage. She chewed at the corner of her lip, butterflies battling inside her stomach.

"Hey, great job today," Bucks voice came back through her phone.

"Thanks." Everleigh smiled.

The wait was killing her. Would he ask? Wouldn't he? Maybe she should just ask. It was the twenty-first century, after all. She squeezed her eyes shut and asked before she could change her mind.

"So, any plans tonight?" It came out rushed and slightly slurred, but at least she'd asked.

"Actually," Buck hesitated, "I have special dinner plans tonight."

"Oh." Everleigh's eyes popped open. "That...that sounds nice."

"I hope it will be. Hey, commercial's almost over. I gotta go. Same time tomorrow?"

"You bet."

Everleigh slid the phone in her purse and creaked her door open to the chilly outside air. Wrapping her arms tightly to her chest, she sagged against the car. She focused on steadying her breathing.

So, today wasn't the day. But that didn't mean tomorrow couldn't be. Or the next day. There was something between her and Buck, she just knew it. Besides, maybe the dinner was with his mother or long-lost uncle.

Shaking out her arms and rolling her shoulders, she didn't bother with locking the car before heading across the street. This early, there weren't many cars out and about, but she recognized the one parked outside Cup of Cheer.

"Go towards the light." She chuckled to herself and hurried towards the warm glow of the coffeeshop.

The chimes above the door jingled as she pushed inside. The scents of sweet pastry dough and coffee were ambrosia to her senses.

"Morning, Deb," Everleigh called out to her boss, who sat at a back table reading the newspaper.

"Morning," came Deb's gruff voice.

"Hey, Mindy." Everleigh forced a smile and chipper attitude for the owner of Cup of Cheer. "Lovely morning, isn't it?"

"Sure is." Mindy smiled as she wiped down mugs. "Just heard you on the morning show. You and Buck ever going to, you know, go on a date?"

"What makes you ask that?" Everleigh's cheeks flushed. They flirted off the air, but she thought they did a pretty good job keeping it professional when others were listening.

"I can feel the chemistry between you two through the radio waves." Mindy laughed. "I think we all can."

"We all?" Everleigh laughed this time. "You two are probably the only ones awake at this hour to listen."

"You might be surprised. People really like to listen to you guys. I mean, you've got people writing in questions and everything."

"Pretty sure that's just Buck making stuff up for the show." Everleigh looked at Mindy skeptically.

"Pretty sure it isn't," Deb commented without putting down her paper.

"Oh, and who's the special gift for?" Mindy leaned in over the counter. "Is it for Buck?"

"What? No." Everleigh waved off that idea. "It's for our Secret Santa exchange at work."

"Seriously?" Mindy leaned back shaking her head.

"What? I love Secret Santa." Everleigh sighed and pulled her neon pink thermos out of her purse. "Can I just get my usual please? I need some caffeine in me before all these questions."

"I'm pretty sure you're the living equivalent of caffeine," Mindy said jealously as she took the thermos and turned to the back counter to start her drink. "I'd kill for your energy."

That put a smile on Everleigh's face as she joined Deb, who, as usual, didn't bother to lower her paper. Everleigh flicked it as she sat down across the table.

"So, what happened yesterday?" She sat her chin in her palm looking at the front-page, yesterday's date gracing the top corner.

Deb lowered the paper just enough to glare at her before raising it again to continue reading. They were up so early that they beat the paper deliveries and Deb was always stuck reading day-old papers. For someone who prided themselves on being on top of local happenings, weather, and all things newspaper worthy, it was the bane of their morning coffee to always be a day behind.

"What?" Everleigh sat back in her chair. "I'd genuinely like to know. You're my main source of serious news."

"That's just sad." Deb finally sat the paper on the table and took a sip of coffee from the plain white mug at her elbow. She finally looked long enough to take in Everleigh's hair and festive accessories and waved a hand up and down in Everleigh's direction. "It's too early for all of this."

Where Everleigh loved color and fun, Deb wore the standard, blue postal uniform every day. Everleigh tried to think of a time when she'd seen her in something else, and nothing came to mind. Even once at church, Deb showed up in full uniform, claiming she had extra work to do afterwards. The thought of a closet stuffed with drab, scratchy blue uniforms made Everleigh shudder.

"I am a treat, and you know it." Everleigh gave her cutest smile. "Work would be way less entertaining without me there to liven it up."

"If you'd just wear a uniform it'd save me time at evaluations." Deb picked up her mug and stared at her over the rim. "And you'd have gotten your yearly raises."

"Some things are more important in life than money. Like personal identity."

"Are we having this conversation again?" Mindy shook her head as she set Everleigh's thermos on the table, along with a bagel.

"Morning tradition." Everleigh smiled and took a giant bite, careful to not smear cream cheese on her perfect lipstick job.

Deb harrumphed and lifted the paper again. Mindy stood at the edge of the table, fiddling with her fingers.

"Um, so, I was wondering if you could help me with something?" She asked in a lowered voice, but Deb still flipped the edge of her paper down to listen.

"Of course. Anything, Mindy. What do you need?"

"So, there's a singles thing at the diner tonight." Mindy wrung her hands and kneeled down next to the table. "And I thought, you know, since you're the most fashionable person I know, maybe you could help me get ready after work?"

"How have I not heard of this?" Everleigh wondered briefly before the weight of what Mindy was asking sunk in. She sucked in a breath. "And are you...are you asking for a makeover?"

"Do I need one?" Mindy ran a hand through her short blonde bob.

"No. You're absolutely perfect." Everleigh beamed and booped Mindy's nose. "We can just add a little make-up, some glitter obviously. I have my travel make-up kit in the Fiesta."

"Ok. Ok." Mindy stood and laughed. "So, you'll help? You could always come, too. I mean, you already look fabulous."

"Sure. I'm always down for moral support." Her heart pinched as she thought of Buck. "And hot cocoa. I assume there will be hot cocoa?"

"Um, of course."

"I'll pop over after work, and we'll get you all festive-ified."

"That sounds perfect." Mindy reached out and gave her hand a quick squeeze. "Thank you, Everleigh. You are a gem."

"See?" Everleigh looked at Deb. "She gets me."

"Well, as fun as this is, it's time to get going." Deb drained the last from her mug and stood. "The mail waits for no man or makeover."

"I'll get those coffees for you right away." Mindy disappeared back around the counter and reappeared moments later with four large, cardboard to-go carafes on a tray.

"Thanks, Mindy." Deb stood and dusted off her pants. "We will all enjoy this today."

"Ohhh...are these for the Secret Santa party?"

"Yep." Deb went to the counter to pay.

"Oh, let me help." Everleigh stuffed her thermos in her purse and her bagel in her mouth so she could carry two of the carafes.

She waved a pinkie at Mindy as they headed out the front door. She made it about two steps onto the sidewalk and hit a patch of black ice. Her normally infallible boots lost their grip and she started to slide, the coffee in each hand windmilling as she tried to keep her balance. The bagel flew from her mouth as she screeched. One carafe flew into the air as her feet slid in opposite directions. The other carafe ended up beneath her as she came down. Her eyes widened as it crunched, and warm liquid covered her legs. She raised her hands just in time to block the falling one from colliding with her head, but the coffee poured out down her sweater.

Everleigh sat for a moment inhaling the French vanilla scent around her, thankful it was at least a flavor she enjoyed.

"Oh my gosh, are you ok?" Deb rushed over, setting the other two carafes on a nearby bench. "You're completely soaked. Did you pull anything? Do you hurt anywhere?"

"No, no. I'm fine." Everleigh reached out for Deb's hand ,and she helped pull her up off the ground. Coffee ran down her skin inside her sweater and down her legs. "Well, that is a strange, but not unpleasant feeling."

"What?"

"It's warm. And it smells nice." Everleigh shrugged.

"Only you would see the bright side to being soaked with coffee, outside, in the middle of winter. You're sure you're ok?"

"Yes. I'm totally fine.' Everleigh chuckled and pulled her sweater away from her body with a sucking sound. "Good thing I keep an emergency change of clothes in my work locker."

"Let's get you in your car before that freezes and turns you into a coffee popsicle."

Deb ushered her across the street and into the Fiesta. Everleigh pulled her emergency blanket from the back seat to sit on. The last thing her car needed was a coffee-soaked driver's seat added to its list of issues.

The drive to the post office was short since it was located one block off town square. Everleigh wrapped herself in the blanket and gently grabbed the wrapped gift off the passenger seat. Shuffling inside, she prayed the other carriers wouldn't be in the locker room. Her boots squelched as she hurried through the back door to the small room with five metal cubbies. She opened hers expecting to find a stack of clothes on the top shelf but found it empty.

"Oh no." Everleigh recalled the jelly doughnut incident from the past week. "Oh no. Oh no."

"Are you all sorted in here?" Deb poked her head around the corner.

"No. No, I'm not." Everleigh plopped down onto the bench that ran along the wall. "I don't have any extra clothes. I used my change last week and forgot to replace it."

"Well, I can't let you go out in the cold soaked from neck to toe in coffee." Deb sighed and disappeared down the hall.

Everleigh let her head fall back against the wall and closed her eyes. What a morning this was turning out to be. Soon, she heard heavy steps return. The click of a hanger and rustle of fabric let her know Deb had returned. She opened her eyes to find a scratchy, drab blue uniform hanging from her open locker door.

"Just put it on and get out here," Deb said as she closed the door.

"What?"

"Just do it," Deb called from down the hall.

"Seriously?" Everleigh looked at the uniform with disgust, but knew she had no other choice. "Ughhhhh."

After locking the door, she peeled off her coffee-soaked clothes. The sweater weighed twice as much as when she'd put it on that morning. The felt elf shoe covers on her boots were totally ruined and went in the trash can. A gag left her throat as she pulled on the stiff dark blue uniform pants and calf high socks.

"Nope. I can't do it." She shook her head when she pulled the shirt off the hanger. "How can they do this every day? Blue with black, really?"

"Everleigh, hurry up in there," Deb hollered down the hall. "We need to get these packages out."

She shoved her arms through the sleeve, the fabric rough against her skin and stiff with newness.

She glanced in the mirror on the back of the door, her nose scrunching. The only positive was that her hair and makeup had made it out unscathed, and from the neck up, she still looked normal. Too bad that was such a small portion of her body.

She made her way out of the locker room and down the hall, tugging at the pants and shirt the entire way to the breakroom. Since her bagel was somewhere on the sidewalk in front of the coffeeshop, she grabbed a package of peanut butter crackers to tide her over until lunch. The dry crackers felt and tasted like sawdust as she made her way back to the loading bay.

"Whoa ho ho," Murray, the other carrier, said when he spotted her. "What do we have here? Is that a uniform I see?"

"There was an incident with two carafes of coffee, some black ice, and my boots." Everleigh held her chin high as she made her way over to the large loading docks. "Coffee that was supposed to be for all of you, I might add. So, double bummer because you don't get coffee and I'm stuck in this monstrosity."

"I'm not sure how I feel about you calling my outfit a monstrosity," Murray joked.

"You pull it off wonderfully, Murray." Everleigh tried to smile but was sure it came out as more of a grimace. "I just prefer more color. And fabric that doesn't feel like sandpaper."

"Wash it a few times and problem solved." Murray patted her shoulder as they walked out into the back parking lot. "Gonna be a long day. More packages than I've ever seen."

"Great."

It would be one of their longest workdays of the year due to all the holiday packages, and she was stuck wearing a boring, uncomfortable uniform. She kicked at the tire of her delivery truck with a sigh.

"Ah, there you are." Deb's feet crunched on the gravel in the parking lot. "The party is scheduled for four this afternoon. If you don't think you'll be finished by then, call in. We may have to help each other out today to get done in time."

"Sounds like a plan." Murray saluted them and climbed into his truck. He backed out slowly and waved out the window.

"It's just one day, Ev," Deb said as they watched him drive away.

"But why today?" Everleigh whined and sagged against the side of her truck. "This is the time of year to be festive and fun."

"Well, I'm pretty sure someone I know has told me many, many, many times that she knows how to put the fun in functional."

Deb cocked an eyebrow at her, turned on her heel, and headed back inside. Everleigh straightened up. She had said that. Probably hundreds of times.

"There will be no wallowing in self-pity today, girl." She pushed up her sleeves and slid open her truck door. "I do put the fun in functional."

Everleigh quickly became engrossed in organizing her truck and schedule. She moved the packages for the diner to the top of the list since they were having the singles event that night. The truck warmed up slowly as she went through the list a final time, checking off boxes and letters for each location.

As she pulled out of the driveway on the way to the diner, she thought of all the nicely wrapped boxes, thinking of what they could be. Gifts from family living far away? Something to wrap up and give to a loved one? An indulgent treat someone got for themselves?

She turned onto Main Street and took it to the town square. Wonderful Thyme sat at the far end, twinkling lights blinking along the edges of their awnings. Everleigh waved as she passed Skye pulling out a book cart and opening her bookstore. Lights were clicking on in most shops along the square, and Everleigh's heart fluttered with pride. This little town of theirs was something truly magical, especially at Christmas.

The diner was open for breakfast, so Everleigh pulled around to the side where they had a delivery door. She crawled into the back of the truck and pulled down the packages to take inside. She hopped out the rear door and shuffled over to the building, eyeing the ground for more black ice. The last thing her backside needed was another spill onto the hard concrete. After knocking, she waited and hoped someone would actually answer. The diner was on her normal route, and she knew they didn't usually take deliveries until after ten.

The door finally opened slightly. Everleigh leaned to the side and waved at the eye peeking through the crack.

"Oh, it's you Everleigh." An old gentleman pushed the door open the rest of the way. "What are you doing here so early? We weren't expecting you until later."

Everleigh grabbed a few of the smaller boxes from the back of the truck and rushed inside. It wasn't nearly as cold as yesterday, but it was still early morning in December, which always meant chilly. She followed him into a small hallway behind the kitchen and placed the packages on the table.

"Morning, Nico. I thought I'd drop yours off a little earlier today since you have the event tonight. Wasn't sure if there was something on my truck you need."

She turned on her heel and ran back out to the truck to grab several larger boxes. Luckily, they were nice and light. She backed into the hallway, pushing the door open with her foot. Hushed whispers came from the far end of the hall.

"...what event, amore?" Nico was asking his wife, Marta.

"What are you talking about?" Marta turned and saw Everleigh. "Oh, yes. The singles event tonight. It should be a magical evening. We will be seeing you, right my dear?"

"Singles event?" Nico threw up his hands and shuffled into the kitchen, muttering to himself.

"I wouldn't miss it." Everleigh hoped her voice sounded genuine. "I'm surprised I hadn't heard about it before today."

"Oh, it was a last-minute plan, cara mio." Marta stopped fussing with packages and looked at Everleigh with a frown. "What is this you're wearing today?"

"The uniform," Everleigh said flatly.

"This is not like you." Marta placed a hand on Everleigh's arm. "Is everything ok?"

"Oh, yeah. Just had a coffee spill this morning."

"Haven't we all." Marta squinted and tilted her head, thinking. "Wait a minute. I have something to liven that up."

Marta disappeared into the office at the end of the hall. Everleigh leaned a hip on the table and peeked into the box Marta opened. An arrangement of holly and ivy with brilliant red berries sat wrapped in a nest of bubble wrap.

"Awww...my favorite!" Everleigh said loudly. "Poinsettias are beautiful, but holly and ivy hold a special place in my heart. And are so underrated. Is it for the event tonight?"

"It sure is." Marta walked slowly out of her office, a green and silver scarf in her hands. "I'm glad you like it."

She smiled and threw the scarf around Everleigh's neck. She fussily tied it and rearranged it. When she was satisfied, she stood back with a nod.

"There you go. Now you look a little more like yourself." Marta sounded proud. "And it matches your wreath earrings."

"Marta. You are so sweet." Everleigh pressed her palm to her chest. "Thank you."

"Of course. You must be busy today."

"So busy." Everleigh's eyes widened.

"Do you want some coffee? Oh, sorry. Probably had enough of that today, huh?" Marta snickered at her own joke. "How about a muffin for the road?"

"I'd never turn down one of your muffins."

Moments later, Everleigh returned to her truck with a comfy scarf and delicious treat. As she spent the morning delivering packages and letters across Reverence Ridge, she tried to be her usual upbeat self. But between the uncomfortable uniform and her thoughts bouncing back to Buck and his dinner plans, she felt distracted. After missing several letters and having to double back, she knew she needed a change. She couldn't show up at the Secret Santa party being a sourpuss. She just couldn't.

As she returned to a house for the second time to deliver a letter she'd misplaced, her phone rang. Deb's name flashed on the screen.

"Hey, Deb," Everleigh tried to sound chipper.

"That doesn't sound good."

Apparently, her chipper was broken.

"Ugh. I'm just a little off my game today."

"In the ten years I've known you, I can count on one hand the number of days you've been off your game." Deb's voice lost its urgent edge as she shifted into her mother hen roll. "Is this about more than the coffee spill?"

"Well, sorta." Everleigh gnawed at her lip and pulled out her sack lunch. Since she was parked, it was as good a time as any for a quick bite. "It's Buck. I really thought today would be the day he'd ask me out."

"I'm pretty clueless in the ways of men, but I can tell you one thing. He'd be a fool to let you go."

"Thanks Deb." Everleigh sighed.

"So," Deb cleared her throat, "how are the deliveries coming? Everyone else is on track to be done and back by four. Do you need help?"

"No, ma'am. I've got this." Everleigh felt a new surge of determination. "I will get everything out on time. You can count on me."

"I have no doubt you will."

The thought of the Secret Santa party was enough to push her through her afternoon deliveries with no more mistakes. She pulled into the back lot at the post office right behind Murray. They smiled and waved as he walked past towards the loading bay doors. Everleigh quickly went through her check list and bolted inside, the annoyance of the uniform momentarily forgotten.

No one was in the locker room when she ducked in to grab her gift. Marta's scarf was too warm to keep tied around her neck, but she undid it and left it draped over her shoulders to cover as much of the uniform as possible. After a quick refresh of lipstick and an extra dab of glitter, she deemed herself ready to party and headed down the hallway.

Hushed voices waited for her in the breakroom. With Deb as their manager, two sorters, and two carriers, there were five employees at the Reverence Ridge post office. Her fellow carriers and sorters waited at the small circular table in the center of the room. A scraggly tree sat in the corner. Everleigh had done everything she could to make it shine, but even her skills had their limits. She reached out to adjust one of the five shining stars she'd crafted out of paper and glitter paint.

"Nice," said Murray. "A shooting star."

"Comet," Everleigh said as she adjusted another. "I'd rather be a comet. A shooting star is a one hit wonder. A comet keeps coming back."

"Well, look at you," Deb said as she walked into the room with a package. "You made it through the whole day."

"Don't get used to this." Everleigh flopped into the last open chair and sat her gift on the table.

Deb actually smiled, which lifted Everleigh's spirits enough that she pulled herself up to the table to watch as the first three gift exchanges, consisting of booze, wacky games, and a cross-stitch kit. Everleigh smiled when she realized it was just her and Deb left, meaning they got gifts for each other. When it was her turn, she pushed her box across the table to Deb.

"Merry Christmas, boss."

Deb tore off the wrapping and opened the box. She pulled out a stack of paper and flipped through the pages.

"I'm not following. It's a list, but of what?"

"The newspaper delivery guy's schedule." Everleigh tapped her fingers together. "Look at what's in the first spot."

"Reverence Ridge." Deb read out. "Ok?"

"I have spent the last three weeks working with him on rearranging his schedule so he can get to Cup of Cheer first in the mornings. I was actually able to shave off 25 miles of driving for him every day. And make sure you get today's paper today. Well, starting tomorrow."

"What? You did all that?"

"Of course, I did. You take good care of us, boss. We take good care of you."

"Um. I don't even know what to say." Deb stood up and came around the table. "Thank you. I can't even wrap my head around how you did it."

"I just called and asked." Everleigh shrugged, looking up at Deb. "He didn't want to hear me out at first, but when I told him I could save him mileage, he was all ears."

"You definitely have the gift of gift giving, or whatever you and Buck were talking about this morning."

"You listen?" Everleigh gasped.

"Hard to miss when Mindy blasts it around the coffee shop everyday." Deb cleared her throat and was all business once more. "Now, here's your gift. Merry Christmas."

She thrust a package into Everleigh's lap and returned to her seat across the table. The wrapping was a bright yellow with green elf legs in different dancing positions. Just looking at it brightened Everleigh's mood. She gently tore at the tape on one end, not wanting to rip the fun paper.

"Oh, just open it already," Deb chided.

"Ok ,ok. It's just such happy wrapping."

"I figured you'd say something like that." Deb stood and walked across the hall. She returned seconds later with the rest of the roll. "There you go. Go crazy."

"Alright." Everleigh shimmied in her seat and then tore into the package in front of her.

Once the paper was off, she lifted the lid on the box and pulled aside the tissue paper. Inside the box lay a button-down shirt cut in the same style as the uniform she was wearing, but the fabric was a bright red covered in little winged envelopes. A post office patch was sewn above the front pocket. Her breath caught in her throat as she pulled it from the box. The fabric flowed across her fingers, not like the stiff company shirts that could practically standup by themselves.

As she held it up, a paper slid out onto the floor. She picked it up and gasped. Her hand flew to her mouth as her eyes darted to Deb, who was actually smiling. Again. Two in one day was unheard of.

"I also spent the last few weeks pulling a few strings." She cleared her throat and adjusted in her seat. "I was tired of docking points on your yearly evaluation. More work for me, you know. So, I found some loopholes and got you official permission to have your own uniforms made."

"You did all that?" Everleigh bounded around the table and threw her arms around Deb's shoulders from behind. "You are amazing. Best Secret Santa ever. Hands down."

"Ok. Ok." Deb chuckled and patted at Everleigh's arms before pushing them off her shoulders.

The five of them spent the next few minutes sipping coffee and munching on pastries. Everleigh hugged her new uniform shirt to her the entire time, just waiting for the opportunity to change into it. When it was finally time to head out, Everleigh rushed back to the locker room and tugged off the traditional uniform. She slid into her new shirt with a sigh. The fabric felt so soft against her skin. Someone knocked at the door, and it opened a crack.

"Kristen and the girls over at Let it Sew made up a pattern to keep on file so you can have them made out of whatever fabric works for you." Deb said, peeking her head in. "Headquarters just asked you keep the cut the same and have the patch sewn on each one."

"That sounds heavenly. I think I'm going to need to go fabric shopping." Everleigh jumped from foot to foot, excited at the thought of a whole new work wardrobe. "Seriously, best Secret Santa ever. Eeek!"

"Good." Deb gave a quick nod and cleared her throat. "And thanks again for what you did with Jack, the paper delivery man. It means a lot."

"Of course." Everleigh did a quick turn in the mirror. "You know, these pants aren't actually that bad."

"Seriously?" Deb sounded exasperated as she stepped back into the hallway. "Ten years you've been fighting me on this and one day in the pants and they're suddenly 'not that bad'..."

Everleigh laughed as Deb's words trailed off towards her office. She pulled on her coat, grabbed her purse, and hurried out to the Fiesta. Mindy would be waiting for her by now. After several attempts, the car started and she was off down the road, huddled over the steering wheel to keep warm. The heater kicked in just as she was parking outside Cup of Cheer.

"Job well done, as usual." She patted the wheel and turned to the backseat and dug through the clothes, food wrappers, books, and other necessary items to find her emergency makeup kit.

It was getting colder now that the sun was disappearing behind the mountains. Inside, the coffee shop was bustling with people in need of warm beverages. Everleigh skirted around the line, waving at the two baristas behind the counter, and made her way back to Mindy's office.

"Is someone here in need of a makeover?" She sang as she opened the door.

"I thought you said I didn't need a makeover," Mindy deadpanned from in front of her computer.

"Hmmm...perhaps 'makeover' isn't the right word." Everleigh air quoted the word. "Sprucing up? A little Christmas tree humor for you. No? Um, how about just getting ready for an evening out? Yeah? Ok. Let me try that again."

Everleigh backed out and closed the door. She cleared her throat and rolled her shoulders before bursting back inside.

"Who wants to get ready for a night out on the town?"

"Me! Me!" Mindy hopped in her seat and raised her hand.

Both of them burst into giggles. Everleigh got to work setting out her makeup on Mindy's desk. They decided a warm color palate would look more natural and make Mindy's blue eyes pop. Everleigh filled her in on the coffee spill accident as she applied brown and gold eyeshadow and mascara. A simple bronzer highlighted her sharp cheekbones and a dusky pink lipstick set off her lips.

"All done. Unless you want a little glitter." Everleigh sounded hopeful as she shook a small bottle of gold sparkles.

"Does anyone ever turn down glitter?" Mindy closed her eyes as Everleigh began applying the glitter over her eyeliner. "I'm really loving the new uniform shirt, by the way. It's very you."

"Thank you." She stuck out her hip, striking a pose, before continuing with the glitter. "It was my Secret Santa gift, if you can believe it."

"That's some Secret Santa."

"Yep. Deb's a real peach."

Mindy disappeared into the employee bathroom to change. Everleigh sat in front of the small mirror and touched up her own make-up, adding a simple cat eye with a silver metallic eyeliner. She pulled her long brown hair out of the pigtails and arranged it into a curly heap on the back of her head. Since she didn't have time to go home and change, her new uniform would have to work. Besides, she loved the new shirt so much she wanted the chance to show it off.

Mindy came out in a simple black pant suit that accentuated her trim figure; her short blonde hair slicked back.

"Dang girl. You look fierce."

"Yes." She snapped her fingers and then slid her arm through Everleigh's. "I plan to slay tonight."

"Sleigh? A little Santa humor?"

"Unintentional, but yes. We'll roll with it."

They hurried through the coffeeshop, which was mostly empty now. They waved to the baristas and headed outside. Night had already fallen, which happened early this time of year. The diner was directly across the square, its large windows casting squares of light on the sidewalk out front. Arm in arm, they slowly meandered towards it, stopping to gaze at window decorations, book carts, and display tables outside shops.

Everleigh could hear Christmas music floating softly from the diner, but oddly, there were no cars out front. Were they early? She shrugged. That didn't bother her. She enjoyed setting up as much as a party itself. Besides, the thought of going to a singles mixer while Buck was out on his special dinner didn't sit well with her. They weren't together, shoot they'd never even gone on a date, but she doubted any other single guy in Reverence Ridge could make her feel what she did every morning when his velvety voice came over the radio.

"I don't know if I'm really feeling the mingling vibe tonight." She stopped just short of the entry way.

"That's ok. I know I kind of sprung this on you." Mindy patted her hand. "Be my wing woman?"

"Oh, boy will I ever." Everleigh sent her friend a thankful smile. "You're going to have so many guys coming your way, like Santa with cookies on Christmas Eve. Sooooo many. I mean, if any show up. What's up with this empty parking lot?"

"Oh, we're just a little early. Thought we could help Marta."

"You're the best."

They walked into the smell of marinara and garlic bread. Everleigh glanced around the diner. She loved the vintage feel, with the red vinyl booths and metal tables. It suited the Christmas feeling perfectly. Marta stood at the back, next to their party room.

"Back here girls." Marta wore all black, her chunky no-slip shoes blending into her work pants. She reached up to give them each a hug when they made their way to the closed door. "Hello, my dears."

"Marta, I'm pulling Wing Woman duty tonight. We are going to make our Mindy girl shine."

"I think you shine wherever you go, cara mio." Marth grasped onto her arm with a grin. "Why don't you head in and see what we've done with the place? My decoration could always use your creative eye. Mindy, come help me get the food ready."

Everleigh opened the door and gasped. Red tapestries hung from the ceilings, covering the walls and making the room feel small and intimate. White poinsettia, roses, and lilies covered every surface, cascading down tiers set in the corners. A single table in the middle of the room shimmered under a chandelier. Candles burned in gilded candle sticks, illuminating gold-edged china place settings. In the center of the table sat the holly and ivy arrangement she'd seen that morning.

"Wow," Everleigh whistled. "Talk about romantic. I don't think anyone could leave this room alone."

"That's what I'm hoping."

A deep, sultry voice came from behind her. Her breath hitched and her eyes widened for a moment. She turned to find Buck behind her holding a single white lily. He wore a plaid button-down shirt tucked into dark slacks. His dark eyes twinkled, and he walked over to her.

"How's my favorite lady this evening?"

"I'm great," she responded, her voice sounding breathier than usual. "How are you?"

"Better now that you're here." He held out the lily for her with a devilish grin.

"Did you...Did you plan all this?"

"A wise woman told me that with a little thought, anyone can give the perfect gift." Buck offered his elbow and led her towards the table.

"Tell me more about this wise woman." Everleigh leaned into him and sighed.

"She's a real live-wire, I tell ya. Always has the answers." Buck teased before his voice softened. "And she's one of the most caring and beautiful women I've ever met."

"Oh, Buck." Her cheeks heated as she slid into the chair he pulled out for her. He sat across from her and folded his hands over his plate. "Did you...comb your beard for this?"

"Only the best for you, Everleigh." He chuckled, stroking his deep red beard.

Mindy and Marta appeared, both wearing red aprons over their black shirts. One carried a bowl of pasta, the other garlic bread. Mindy winked as she placed the bowl on the table.

"You were all in on this!"

"Of course, we were." Mindy laughed.

"We just want you to be happy, cara mio." Marta said softly. She turned to Buck and her eyes hardened. "If you hurt her, you'll have to answer to us."

"Only the best intentions here, ladies. I promise." Buck sat back and held his hands up in surrender.

"Ok, ok. Let's leave it at that before we get to real threats." Everleigh stood and ushered them both out of the room, closing the door behind them. She made her way back to her seat and steepled her hands under her chin. "Now, where were we?"

"How you deserve only the best."

"No. No. I think we were at you combing your beard."

"I thought maybe we could move past that without further comment."

"Hm. I'll consider it since you went to all this work."

Buck leaned over the table and held out a hand. She leaned forward and slid hers into his, and he rubbed his thumb over her knuckles.

"So, you were talking about love languages this morning." He cleared his throat. "I believe when I asked what yours was, you said, 'Wouldn't you like to know.' Well, I would like to know. Will you tell me now?"

She sighed, leaning her head onto her other fist. His words flowed over her like warm honey.

"My love language? I'm pretty sure it's anything you say, Buck. Just keep talking."

Warrick

T he back fields called to him, urging him further through the trees. Warrick revved his four-wheeler, the bitter wind biting into his cheeks. His border collie dodged branches next to him, her tongue lolling for the first run of the day. The sky was just turning from velvety black to smokey gray as he crested a hill. Tree covered mountains lay before them, behind them, all around them.

They stopped next to a large, flat rock at the very crest of the mountain. It had been his favorite place since he was big enough to drive the four-wheeler, maybe eight years old. He'd been bringing Pondarosa there since she was a pup so small he had to hold her in his lap. He grabbed the thermos and pulled himself up to his usual spot. With his legs dangling over the edge, he stared as the sun crested the mountaintops in front of him, brilliant reds, pinks, and oranges. Pondarosa sat next to him, leaning in and licking his ear. After tugging off a glove with his teeth, he opened his thermos and took a long drink of steaming coffee, then buried his fingers in Pondarosa's thick, soft fur.

"One more week, Rosa. We just have to get through one more week." He ruffled her ears. "Then we can sleep for a month."

She huffed and shook her head, tags jingling in disagreement.

"Ok, ok." He laughed quietly. "I'll sleep. You keep an eye on everything for me."

Pondarosa pushed her nose under his fingers, licking them before rolling onto her back. Warrick used both hands to scratch her belly as she squirmed in delight.

"Alright girl, time to work." He capped his thermos and pushed himself up as she bounded off the back of the rock. "Man, what I'd give for a portion of your energy."

All he got in return was a string of barks as she disappeared into the trees to the north. Soon, he was on her tail with the four-wheeler, racing towards their Fraser Fir lot. With only one week until Christmas, their tree farm was booming, and Fraser's were their most popular tree variety. They also happened to be in the farthest lot from the house.

After crossing the road they used to divide the tree varieties, he slowed down and held out a hand. The pine branches slid over his fingers, and he veered off to the east where their oldest trees were. He had a daily quota to cut before opening, which meant he was out before the sun came up and went to bed long after it went down. They had a strict system for cutting trees and always took the oldest before they got too big. In spring they would be out here pulling stumps and planting new seedlings. They worked all year to get these four weeks' worth of business in December.

Pondarosa appeared as he parked next to the final row. Her rich brown fur was covered with pine needles and dirt.

"Find a good spot to roll in?" Warrick pulled a chainsaw from the trailer attached to the ATV. He leaned down to pick out a few pine needles, but Pondarosa hopped away. "Fine, keep them, but you know Mama won't let you in the house like that."

It almost looked like she rolled her eyes as she stopped to shake off the majority of the dirt and debris. Warrick turned his head to smile and looked down the row. Fraser Firs tended to grow far slower than other varieties, at maybe a foot a year. This row was planted almost a decade ago, giving them a nice variety between five and nine feet tall, which was perfect for most houses.

Warrick put in his earbuds and cranked the music from his phone. He slid his safety goggles from his front pocket and primed the chainsaw. With a pull of the cord, the engine came to life. It purred as he laid down on his side next to the first tree. The blade bit into the trunk and sliced cleanly through. Warrick held onto the branches with one hand and turned off the saw with the other. The tree fell behind him as he began to drag it toward the trailer. Once it was laid inside the rails, he went back to do the same with the next one.

The trailer was full when he tossed the seventh tree on the top and he'd worked up a sweat already. Pondarosa hopped up onto the seat behind him, and they set off towards the barn. The air rushing over him cooled him down quickly, leaving him cold by the time they made it out of the trees.

Their wooden barn stood dark next to their house in the early morning light. He pulled around back and opened the loading door. He hefted the trees off the trailer and leaned them against the railings they had set up in the corner. They would be trimmed and put through the shaker before being moved to the sales floor later that afternoon. He needed to make one more trip before breakfast, then the family would come work in the barn while he made a couple more trips out to the tree lots.

At least the next batch wouldn't be as far out. The White Firs were in a lot on the west side and much closer to the house. He'd be able to pull a batch of those and be back before his wife, Whitney, had breakfast on the table and his parents showed up to help.

"White Firs next, girl," he hollered at Pondarosa as he hopped back on the four-wheeler.

The sun overhead twinkled through the branches of the massive trees growing directly behind their house. They took the brunt of the cold northern winds, keeping the house and barn warm and peaceful. Their property was at the edge of the valley Reverence Ridge sat in. Beyond the immense trees edging their yard, it became rocky and hilly. Steep rises and deep ravines were common, but Warrick knew this land like the back of his hand. He breezed past the tall trees with Pondarosa trotting behind, tongue flapping in the wind. The trailer bounced behind him, jerking his four-wheeler backwards.

"Come on girl, beat you there." He twisted the throttle to the max, the four-wheeler jumping beneath him at the abrupt change in pace.

Moments like this were what got him through the month of December. Racing through the trees, not another human soul around. Just him and his pup enjoying some wind through their hair. His business might be selling trees, but they were also a balm to his soul. He felt more at home in the wooded mountaintops than he ever did amongst people in town.

He pulled left abruptly before coming up on an impassable outcropping and skidded to a halt. Pondarosa, who raced to catch up, never faltered and launched herself into the seat behind him. She set her chin on his shoulder, licking his ear and keeping an eye out.

His breath came in quick puffs as they slowed their pace and worked their way through a tight patch of wild pines. Once through, their well-plotted lot of White Firs felt spacious and airy.

He made his way to the oldest row and grabbed the saw. He walked down to the end so the closest ones to the trailer would be the easiest to load when he was wearing out. Pondarosa trotted next to him; her ears pinned back.

The chainsaw's starter cord was in his hand when the hair on Pondarosa's neck rose. A low growl rolled from her throat. Warrick quickly set down the saw and grabbed a hunting knife from his belt. He signaled for Pondarosa to stay and unsheathed his blade.

A twig snapped in the cluster of trees. It could be the den of a bobcat or fox, but Warrick didn't think there was anywhere large enough to house a black bear. He was pretty confident this creature would on the smaller side, but that didn't mean they would be any less dangerous. He thought of the nasty gash his buddy got when a wild boar charged him, and his heart ticked up a beat.

Pondarosa barked a warning, baring her teeth. Warrick backed towards the four-wheeler, snapping his fingers towards the seat. Pondarosa's eyes never left the trees as she slowly jumped up.

A sudden flurry of dried leaves flew from the trees, accompanied by low grunting. Adrenaline dumped into Warrick's veins as he turned and sprinted. He made it halfway down the row when his foot sank into a hole. He felt, or maybe heard, a loud popping as he tumbled to the ground. The hunting knife landed under his hand, slicing into his palm, but he didn't have time to think about it. His fingers closed over the handle, and he rolled tohis back, the knife in front of him at the ready.

Pain, hot and immediate, ran up his leg making his vision fuzz as something small and black darted out of the trees. A bear cub? Then he saw the white stripe and fell back with relief. The knife thudded to the ground as he pressed both palms to his forehead. He pulled the cut hand away with a hiss.

"A damn skunk, Rosa?" he hollered.

The dog hopped down from the seat and ran to his side, licking his face, tail wagging the entire time. The little skunk rummaged through some leaves, crunching as it shuffled. Pondarosa tuned with a jump and barked once, sending the skunk rushing back into the brush.

Warrick sat up, wincing as pain seared from his ankle. He poked at the top part of his boot, causing lightning to shoot up his leg. Gasping, he flopped back to the ground. Thin, gray clouds floated overhead as he counted his breaths. With the threat of danger gone, and the adrenaline with it, his limbs felt heavy and exhausted.

The cut on his palm wasn't deep, just a scratch that'd stopped bleeding already, but he was still careful with it as he pressed his fists into his closed eyes, focusing on being calm. Pondarosa nudged his elbow with her nose, whining softly. He reached out and pulled her down next to him, rubbing her soft fur. She licked his arm over and over trying to comfort him.

"Alright, girl. Let's see if we can make it back and get some ice on this." He patted her side and pushed himself up onto his elbows. "Pop a few Advil, and I'm sure we'll be back out here after breakfast."

He sat up and flipped over to his knees. He hopped up onto his good foot, wobbling until he caught his balance. He set his hurt foot out in front of him.

"Hm. So far, so good. Probably nothing."

He put a fraction of his weight down onto his leg and almost collapsed. Blinding white lights pulsed in his vision as he cried out. Swaying, he instantly pulled back onto his good leg. Sweat prickled his brow as Pondarosa whined and pressed into him, offering her support.

"Holy Moses." He panted.

After waiting for the throbbing to subside, he hopped the rest of the way to the four-wheeler. He threw his bad leg over the seat and winced as it bumped against the floorboard. The engine rumbled to life, and he slowly inched back towards the house.

"This is going to be slow going, girl." Warrick gritted his teeth as every bump sent shooting pain up his leg.

Finally, they pulled out of the massive pines and parked between the house and barn, unsure where to go first. Beneath his jacket, his shirt was drenched with sweat and his jaw ached from clenching his teeth so tight.

"There you are. I was about to send out the search dogs," his wife, Whitney, said from the back porch. "Breakfast is on the table."

Warrick didn't say anything, just sat hunched over the handlebars sucking down large gulps of air.

"Did you hear me, Warrick?" She took a few steps off the porch before breaking into a sprint. "Warrick? Oh, God. What's wrong? Warrick?"

"I stepped in a hole." He peeled his hands from the handles and turned to look at her. "My ankle is a little sore. I'll put a little ice on it while we eat and be just fine."

"Right. Let me see." She knelt next to his foot and pulled up the pant leg. "Jesus. It's straining your boot laces it's so swollen. We're going to see Doc."

"Whit, I don't need the doctor. Just help me inside."

"Warrick, if I can tell there's something wrong with it, there's definitely something wrong with it. The instant you take off that boot, you're not even going to be able to get it back on. I'm calling your folks to come feed the kids. We're going. Don't move."

"Not planning on it." He sighed and slumped over the handles. His face pressed against the plastic engine cover as Whitney ran inside. "A damn skunk, Rosa. A skunk."

Whitney came running back a minute later, pulling a coat on over her company shirt and leggings. She jingled the car keys at him as she ran past. Moments later, their truck was sliding up next to him. Whitney left the engine running as she hopped out to help him.

"Your folks are on the way; they'll be here in about five minutes." She pushed him up to sitting and pulled his arm over her shoulders. "Kayla's already up and watching Jackson."

He looked over to the window in their back door and saw Kayla staring back, her red hair still wild from sleep. She gave him a quick wave and hefted Jackson up to see out the window too. Their eyes were wide.

"We can wait. I hate to leave them like this." He settled with both legs over one side of the seat. "They look scared."

"They are scared, babe. Their indestructible Daddy just came home hurt and flopped over the handles of the ATV like an uprooted sapling." She pressed her hands to both sides of his face, forcing him to look at her. "Kayla's entered that pre-teen phase where being in charge is, like, super thrilling. Letting her play mom for all of five minutes will probably be the highlight of her day."

With one last look at the house, he let Whitney help him to the truck. Several colorful words later, he made it to the door. He was able to prop his bad leg on the seat, and with a butt boost from his wife, he slid the rest of him inside with only minor bumping.

His parents' car pulled up next to them, but instead of rolling down the windows to chat like usual, Whitney just waved and threw the truck into gear. Warrick ground his teeth together again as they bounced down their gravel drive. Once they made it to the smooth road, he relaxed slightly and laid back against the headrest.

Several long minutes later, Doctor Allen met them outside his office with a wheelchair, which Warrick tried to refuse, but was shoved into and wheeled inside by his wife.

"So, let's start with hearing what happened." Doctor Allen helped him onto the exam table and sat at the computer, tapping away.

"Pondarosa got spooked. I wasn't sure what it was, so I went to run back to the ATV and stepped in a hole." He was really hoping they wouldn't ask what had spooked her. "I heard- or felt maybe? - a popping when I fell."

"Well, popping can mean a lot of things." Doc scooted over on his stool and pulled his glasses on. "So, let's take a look and see if we can figure it out."

Whitney stood next to the exam table and slid her hand into his as Doc started unlacing his boot. His teeth clamped together so tight he could hear them grinding. The thought passed through Warrick's head that he may need to see a dentist as well when all this was over. He squeezed Whit's fingers and swallowed hard as his boot came off. Doc tsked and slowly pulled off Warren's thick, woolen sock. Whitney gasped lightly as Warren gripped her hand again.

"Sorry, babe," his voice was rough as he loosened his fingers.

"It's ok. You did the same for me through two babies being born." She squeezed his hand back. "I can take it."

Warrick had never been more thankful to have a strong wife as he was over the next few minutes of the doctor examining his ankle and foot. Each touch and movement sent a jolt up his leg and into his back. He gave up on sitting and laid back on the exam table, sweating and shaking by the time Doc was done with his examination.

"Well, that hole did a real doozie to your ankle. With the swelling and some bruising forming on the top of the foot, my educated guess is that you broke the talus, or ankle bone." Doc shifted his glasses to the top of his head. "An x-ray would confirm it, but we'll have to wait for swelling to go down."

"So, what does this mean?" Warrick propped himself up on his elbows. "I've got trees to cut."

"It means someone else will have to cut those trees." Doc crossed his arms. "You need to stay off your foot for at least six to twelve weeks."

"What?" Warrick flew up to sit in front of the doctor. "No. That's not gonna work. Can't you just wrap it up, slap some ice on it, give me some pain killers, and send us on our way?"

"Warrick." Doc Allen lowered his chin, looking at Warrick like he would a temperamental child. "This could be a serious break. If you don't stay off it, you're going to prolong the recovery. Maybe even cause permanent damage."

"Babe, we'll figure this out." Whitney slid closer to his side, rubbing a hand across his shoulders. "Your health is our top priority."

"But...But..." Warrick sputtered, not wanting to believe what he was hearing. "That's two to three months. Months."

"Well, look at the bright side. Maybe this year you won't work yourself to exhaustion and actually be able to celebrate Christmas." Doc shrugged. "Just try to find the silver lining."

"That's true." Whitney gave him a lopsided smile. "It would be nice for you to be around for Christmas. Spend some time with the kids. Join us for dinner with your folks."

"What are you talking about?" Warrick could feel his anger rising. He didn't like being ganged up on. "I do that every year. I'm always there."

"Physically, yes. But you're so exhausted you don't actually do anything." Whitney bit her lip.

"If I remember correctly, was that two years ago, he fell asleep and snored through church service?" Doc chuckled.

"I did what?" Warrick's eyes widened. "I did not."

"Baby, you did." Whitney nodded while cringing.

Warrick crossed his arms over his chest and scowled. So, he was just a joke now? He worked his tail off to provide for his family and the whole town was laughing at him behind his back?

"Don't be upset." Whitney tried to soothe his annoyance. "We just didn't say anything because you work so hard the weeks leading up to Christmas. Everyone knows that."

"So, what now?" He didn't meet either of their eyes.

"I'm going to put a boot on it to keep it immobilized and give you a pair of crutches." Doc stood and walked to the door. "And you're going to stay off it, or I will personally come out and tie you down with some of your fabulous fresh pine garland."

Warrick's mouth fell open as Doc Allen walked out of the exam room. He'd been seeing Doc since he was born, and he didn't remember him ever being anything other than a kind, overly helpful, old man.

"You should see your face." Whitney laughed. Not a small chuckle either. A bend-over-and-slap-your-knee kind of laugh.

"What is happening right now? First Doc threatens me? Now you're laughing at me?" Warrick glanced around the room. "Have I fallen into some kind of alternate dimension of opposites?"

"No, babe." She wiped at her eyes, still catching her breath. "You're just out of your element. Maybe letting other people help you for once will be good for you."

"You make me sound like some kind of control freak workaholic." Warrick lowered his voice and stared at his feet, one in his work boot, the other bare.

"Au contraire." Whitney stepped up, wedging herself between his feet. "You work triple hard to make an easier life for the people you care about. You show your love by doing for others. Relying on only yourself to get the job done has made you into a leader. Both of those things are wonderful and a big part of why I love you."

"Why do I sense a 'but' coming?" He placed his hands on her hips, slipping his thumbs through her belt loops like he'd done a thousand times.

"But...," she drug the word out, "now you need us. And it will be a joy for *us* to do for *you* what you've been doing for so long. Let us take care of you for a change. Ok? Can you do that?"

"Doesn't seem I have much choice."

"There's the spirit!" Whitney wrapped her arms around him and pulled him to her for a hug. "We'll get through this, babe. Who knows, maybe you'll even learn how to relax. Sitting on a rock in the woods long enough for you to take two sips of coffee every morning doesn't count as relaxing."

"Sure, it does." He wrapped his arms around her, too. "It's speed relaxation. Like the awake version of a cat nap."

"Only you, Warrick. Only you."

About a half hour later Warrick was making his way out of the office in a boot and on crutches. He knew after ten steps that the crutches had to go. Coordinating them with his steps and keeping them from hitting chairs and door frames was just too much to bother with. He tossed them in the back end of the truck and hopped to the passenger door. The ride home was silent as he stared out the window, trying to figure a way out of this mess.

When they pulled into the driveway, Pondarosa came barreling out of the barn, her tail wagging a mile a minute. Whitney grabbed onto her collar so he could slide out of the truck onto his good leg without being plowed over.

"Oh yeah, I meant to ask," Whitney said while shushing Pondarosa. "What spooked her out there?"

"Ugh. I was so hoping you'd forget that part." His shoulders sunk. "You can't tell anyone this. Promise?"

"Maybe." Whitney's interest was piqued, and she leaned in.

"It was a skunk."

For the second time that morning, Whitney was bent over with laughter. Warrick thrust his fists onto his hips while leaning against the truck, trying to keep his balance.

"I thought it was a boar or bobcat or something the way she started growling." He tried to talk over her laughter but gave up.

"Oh babe, I love you." She reached out to squeeze his elbow before wiping tears from her eyes. "We can just say it was a small black bear. With a distinctive white stripe."

That set her off on another round of laughter. Warrick left her and hopped across the yard to the porch. Inside the house was empty, meaning his folks and the kids must be over in the barn. He used the counter to balance and ate a couple pieces of cold French toast, shoving whole slices in his mouth.

"Sorry for laughing." Whitney came in behind him as he was washing down the food with a glass of milk. "I found this in the barn for you. Thought you might like it better."

She handed him her dad's old cane. Warrick had made it for him out of one of their own trees, sanded, and polished it to a shine. Her dad had used it in his last few years, then it returned to them when he passed, and it found a home in the barn.

"Thanks. I think I would." He thumped it on the ground, testing it out, then looked her in the eye. "What are we going to do, Whit? How do we get through this?"

"With a little help, my dear." She waved a small blue book at him, the Reverence Ridge phone book. "I've got it all planned out."

She proceeded to tell him about her plan, which involved him manning the gift shop. Before he could but in, she raised a finger to silence him and rushed on. She continued to talk as she helped him make his way to the barn and plunked him in a folding chair behind the counter.

"Now, you just relax here. We'll take care of everything."

And with that she disappeared behind the curtain separating the shop from their tree staging area. Warrick glanced around like he'd never seen this room. He didn't remember the last time he'd done more than poke his head in here. Pondarosa came in and sat at his feet.

"What just happened?" He laid the cane across his lap so he could reach down to pet her. "Is that what I do?"

Did he just took control of the situation and not allow any discussion? Because he did not like what just happened. He felt like he'd been whisked up and plopped down with no say. And now he had to sit here and sell ornaments, fertilizer, and wrapping paper.

After a few minutes, he realized sulking and wallowing wasn't much fun if no one was around to notice. For a few minutes, he hobbled around the small gift shop ,rearranging ornaments into more logical displays. All the reds in one area, silver in another. He stood back with satisfaction just as his mother ducked under the curtain from the back of the barn.

"Rearranging already huh?" She tilted her head and looked at the wall he'd just organized. "I like it better the old way. It was more charming."

Warrick pursed his lips and turned back to the wall and began to re-rearrange everything, mixing it up with no order or thought. He shoved ornaments on the hooks. Reds with blues. Silver next to green. Pickles next to a Christmas Cupid. Reindeer next to a Santa on the beach. It was ornament chaos.

"Looks better already. So, how you holding up?"

"Fine. Just fine." He tried to keep the anger out of his voice but didn't succeed.

"I think this will be good for you, y'know?" His mom flopped into his folding chair and propped her feet up on the counter. She popped the end of a candy cane in her mouth and watched him. "You need some rest."

"That's what January is for," he muttered.

"Yeah, well, maybe you won't sleep through church this year."

"Why?" He threw his hands up and turned to her. "Why is this the first I'm hearing about that?"

"Whitney told me Doc spilled the beans." She chuckled. "So, I can officially give you a hard time about it."

"Thanks. Because that's just what I need today."

"Oh, I'm sorry." Her feet dropped to the floor, and she hurried around the counter, her boots clomping with each step. "Do you need a hug from Mommy? Hm?"

She threw her arms around him with flourish, reaching up to ruffle his hair. In his attempt to protect himself from her onslaught of motherly affection, he lost his balance and hop-toppled back into the ornament wall. Several fell to the floor at their feet.

"Ok, ok." He laughed, gently pushing her arms away. "So, I want a little pity today. Sue me."

"You're right." She straightened her button-down shirt and fixed the collar. "What kind of mother would I be if I didn't support your pity party at least for a little while?"

"Thank you," he said, pulling his shoulders back. "Is that too much to ask?"

"Not at all, Ricky. Why don't you go sit down and I'll clean up this mess you made."

"That I made? Ha. Nice try, Mama." He wasn't going to stand around waiting, so he hopped over to the chair and fell ungracefully into it, boot smacking the floor. He winced and grabbed his leg. "So, what are Whit and Dad doing? I didn't get the full plan."

"Oh, they're in the back talking about cutting down some Frasers. We're pretty low in staging, and today's bound to be busy, being a couple days 'til Christmas and all."

"I better go see if they need help." He pushed out of his chair and through the back curtain.

"Guarantee you they don't," his mother called after him.

Pondarosa cracked an eye open as he left but didn't make a move to follow. Apparently she took him 'relaxing' as a sign she could do the same, which really had him wondering what she actually did all of January.

Using the cane, he hobbled towards the loading door at the back of the barn. He could just make out the hushed voices of Whitney and his dad. They were next to the ATV outside. A helmet dangled from his father's hand.

"You better not be planning on going out there on your own."

They both started and turned.

"What are you doing up?" Whitney's brow creased with concern. "I plopped you in that chair for a reason."

"Ma said you were heading out for Frasers. You still remember the way?" He looked at his dad.

"Do I still remember?" His dad barked a laugh. "Did you forget that I ran this farm for longer than you've been alive, young man?"

"Nope. Just wondering if memory loss has set in yet, old man."

"He remembers just fine." Whitney rolled her eyes at their typical insult exchange. "And he won't be going alone."

"You're not planning to go out there, are you?" Warrick asked.

"No, but why shouldn't I? I've been married to you long enough to know how to cut down a tree, Warrick Sagehorn."

"Never said you couldn't, babe. Just assumed you'd want to be here to run things."

"I plan to be. And don't add to my job today by making me babysit you, too."

"So, then who's going out with Dad? Frasers are the furthest lot." Warrick gestured towards the trees. "I'll hop right on the back of the ATV, Dad. You cut, I'll drag and load."

"No way. You think I want Doc Allen coming after me?" His dad vigorously shook his head. "Besides, I don't need you. The cavalry is here."

His dad raised an arm, pointing towards the end of the driveway. Warrick heard wheels on the gravel. Soon, vehicles started pulling around to park at the back of the barn. Five or six at first, then more. Folks from all over town poured out, waving as they approached.

"Hey, y'all," Whitney hollered and waved them all over. "Thanks so much for coming out."

"We're so excited to help." Birdie Countryman, a friend from church, walked up arm in arm with her husband, Chris.

Jeremy, a young guy from Taylor Calloway's construction crew, was strapping on a toolbelt as he approached. Celia from church was carrying two carafes of coffee and beaming from ear to ear. And the people just kept on coming.

"First things first, who here's comfortable with an ATV and a chainsaw?" Whitney asked.

Several people raised their hands and Whitney organized pairs to head out and restock their tree supply. At first, Warrick tried to cut in to give instructions, but found that as he listened, she gave them all the information they needed. Where the oldest rows were, how to start at the end and work down. Within ten minutes she had all the extra people assigned to different tasks and their farm was bustling and moving like a well-oiled machine.

"Close your mouth, dear." Whitney walked back to him and steered him towards the giftshop. "I told you. We've got this."

"I see that." Warrick looked around him at all the people working in their staging area. "I'm just having trouble believing it."

"Well, believe it, Honey," Whitney sang out. "Mama don't mess around."

"You're amazing, you know that?" He stopped when they reached the curtain. He bent down and kissed her fully on the mouth.

"Yes," she whispered against his lips. "Yes, I do know that. Now, sit. And rest."

She pushed down on his shoulder so he'd sit in the folding chair, and then disappeared back behind the curtain. Tapping the toes on his good foot, he looked around the room. Pondarosa was asleep on her back, legs twitching in the air. Warrick shook his head with a chuckle.

All he could see over the counter was the top of his mom's head, bobbing around the room as she hummed an off-tune version of Carol of the Bells. He could hear laughter from behind him, and it brought a smile to his face. His normal day consisted of trips back and forth to cut whatever they were running low on and helping his dad in the staging area. He never got to stop and see how the business actually ran or interact with customers.

His daughter, Kayla ran into the room, coming to a stop when she saw him. She ran over, gave him a big hug, and without a word, ran out the door. A loudspeaker crackled to life, and soon a chimes version of "We Wish You a Merry Christmas" assaulted his ears. They were officially open for business.

"Good Lord Almighty." He clamped his hands to his ears.

"It's a little louder here than out in the trees, huh?" his mom leaned onto the counter, resting her chin in her hands.

"It's beautiful up in the hills. I always like hearing it. But here? That was just awful."

"Well, don't tell Kayla that. Setting off the opening chimes is her job, and she takes it very seriously."

"You don't say." Another thing he'd somehow missed.

When Kayla came bolting back through the door, he was ready for her. He reached out and pulled her to a stop before she could disappear again.

"So, what's this I hear about you having a job? Isn't eleven too young to be working?"

"Daddy," she giggled. "I've been doing it all year already."

"Well, did you know that hearing those chimes is my absolute favorite thing every morning?" He tugged on her ear. "And now that I know you're the one turning them on, I like them even more."

He let her go, and she disappeared with a massive smile on her face. Moments later, the first customers walked in. His mom instantly assisted them with picking out the perfect tree food and trimmings. When another couple walked in, Warrick hopped around the counter to offer his assistance.

"Hey, do you know about the trees outside?" the man asked.

"I think I know a thing or two." Warrick smiled. "What can I help you with?"

He talked them through selecting the perfect tree variety for their needs, told them how best to take care of it once they got home, and even added a tree stand to the sale. After that couple, another walked through the door. And then another. And before he knew it, the sun was setting outside the barn window, and Warrick had no idea where the day even went. Kayla ran through again and this time he knew to cover his ears before the chimes sounded. They were closed.

"I think you missed your true calling." His mom said from the cash register. She was busy adding up receipts. "We had more sales today than in a long time. All from your up-sales."

"I never thought I'd like being couped up in this room, but, if I'm being honest, I really enjoyed today." Warrick felt a giddy sense of pride in his chest. "Getting to interact with people was actually fun."

"Yeah, it really is." His mom had stopped counting and stared at him.

As soon as she went back to counting, he started tidying up the room and restocking items they'd sold out of. Throughout the day, he'd gotten more comfortable with the cane and the boot didn't feel quite so cumbersome. As he was hanging the last of the bows, a glorious scent filled his nose.

"What is that heavenly smell?" He sniffed again and moaned.

"Dinner." Whitney called from the back of the barn.

He hopped hurriedly through the curtain and stopped short on the other side. Around fifteen people were setting up folding tables and chairs, their chatter and laughter filling the large space. Warm lights glowed overhead, making everything cozy, if a large barn could be called that.

"Well, babe, we did it." Whitney walked up to him with a smile. "And I hear you were the sales team MVP."

"We have a sales team now?"

"Yeah. You and your mom." She nuzzled under his arm. "Isn't it every guy's dream to be on a team with their mom?"

"Maybe not most moms, but my mom can throw down. I'd pick her any day."

"I know you would."

They stood in silence for a few minutes, just watching the people around them.

"I never knew it could be like this," he finally said. "I always thought I was doing everyone a favor."

"Sometimes letting someone do something for you is more of a gift to them."

"I see that."

"Do you really?" Whitney looked deep into his eyes, searching.

"Yes. After seeing all this and all you can do, I don't think I want to go back to our old, lonely ways."

"That would make me really, really happy."

"Maybe I'll even hire some help."

"Chuck over there has been asking about a job all day." Whitney pointed to a gangly kid who looked about fourteen. "Something about job security? I don't know. But he worked his tail off, and I think he'd be a great place to start."

"Yes, ma'am. Seems like we've got a new boss 'round here, too." Warrick tipped an imaginary hat in her direction. "Now what smells so good?"

"The church ladies brought over a baked potato buffet."

Warrick's stomach rumbled in response. He threw an arm around Whitney's shoulders, and they slowly hop-walked towards the food table.

"So, I had some ideas for the gift shop."

"Oh, you did? After one day?"

"Yep. I'm thinking we're going to need to expand. I'm picturing a kids' craft table. And handmade ornaments."

"Whoa. Did you clear that with your boss?"

"Not yet. Think she'll go for it?"

"Who wouldn't go for kids' crafts and handmade ornaments?" She stood up on tiptoe and kissed his cheek. "It's a fabulous idea."

He decided to hold off on sharing his other fabulous ideas. Like letting his dad go out in the trees more often so he could stay in the barn. Or finding something more soothing for the chimes. And making sure he never slept through Christmas church service again.

Viola

V iola yanked the curtains closed, trying to block out the carolers walking down her street. Not that she didn't love an enthusiastic "Here Comes Santa Clause", but she had work to do. She raked her fingers through her hair, and they became ensnared in tangles, making her wonder when she'd showered last. After a quick sniff of her shirt, she decided it had been far too long.

With a yawn, she padded towards the bathroom, where she was struck with options. Take a shower, which is where all the best thinking happened. Or soak in the tub and relax. Did she have the energy for deep thought? Did she have time to relax?

"Ugh," she groaned and slid down the wall, her head falling into her hands. She pulled her knees up to her chest and sat there debating.

For the love, Vi. This is a simple choice. It should not have you curled up on the bathroom floor.

She mentally chided herself, but it wasn't enough to make her get up. Sliding down even further, she sprawled out, pressing her cheek onto the cool tile floor. She hadn't bothered cleaning anything when she moved in a couple months ago and the threat of germs weighed on her. The image of a barefoot stranger standing in that very spot flashed before her eyes and she scrambled up, wiping at her cheek.

But she had so much work to do that cleaning, and unpacking, for that matter, were far down her list of priorities. The only rooms not still stuffed with moving boxes were her bedroom and the sun-room-turned-art-studio.

Just the thought of her art studio had her rushing into the shower, where she thoroughly scrubbed the floor germs off her cheek and conditioned her hair multiple times to work out the tangles. As her hands scrubbed, her mind returned to her art.

How can I fix it?

What's my inspiration?

Will I still have a fan base when I return to the city?

Question after question roared ceaselessly through her mind. Even though showers allowed for the best thinking, she didn't find any answers. Mrs. Bell, her high school art teacher and current mentor, would say 'Art isn't thinking, Viola. It's feeling.'

Maybe that was her problem. When was the last time she felt something? Aside from her crushing anxiety, of course. That was the whole point of her returning to Reverence Ridge. After bopping from one huge city to the next, she needed to get back to her roots. When this adorable bungalow, with its wrap around porch and dreamy sunroom had popped up online for rent, she thought it was a sign that returning home would be her answer. So, she jumped at it, packed up all her stuff, and moved back to Tennessee in the span of a week.

And now she was thoroughly stuck. She'd signed a year long lease using the last of her savings. It didn't matter if she missed the art museums, night life, and architectural inspiration the cities provided. She'd made a spur of the moment decision and now had to deal with the consequences.

Ugh. Adulting sucks.

She pulled on a pair of sweats and the oldest, softest t-shirt she owned, along with some fluffy socks to keep her toes warm. Her hairbrush sat neglected in a bathroom drawer. She pulled it through her hair, easing out the last of the tangles. Then she ran her tongue over her teeth and decided she'd been neglecting another kind of brush for too long as well.

With minty fresh breath, and feeling halfway human again, she made her way through the maze of stacked boxes that was her living room. In the kitchen, she leaned against the counter and stared at the coffee maker as it slowly dripped life-giving liquid into the pot. As she stared at it, her mind wandered back to her art, as always.

What inspired her?

That was the crux of the issue. She had no inspiration. Nothing. Not like her last collection, which gushed out of her in the span of two weeks. Now she was coming up on two years since she'd sold the last of that collection at one of the most niche art galleries in Los Angeles. Almost two years with nothing new to show.

Felix is going to drop you, Vi. You've got to pull it together.

Her agent, Felix Winfield, was one of the most sought-after agents, especially for abstract watercolor painters like herself. He'd seen her work at a city-wide art festival where she'd set up on the side of the street with every other amateur painter in Hollywood trying to sell her paintings for $50 a pop. For some reason she still didn't understand, he'd stopped at her booth and whisked her away to a life of art gallery showings and private auctions where her paintings sold for a hundred times what she'd been asking at that festival.

While she loved the exposure and recognition, the lifestyle was exhausting. Parties would go into the wee hours of the morning every night of the week. Felix had expectations about dress codes for his clients, which was nothing like the sweats and t-shirt she was snuggled in now. In fact, if he saw her now, he'd do his signature showing of distaste, where he had an arm across his chest, tapped his chin with his other hand, and curled up one side of his lip. He didn't need to say a word to let you know that you were far below his standards.

I wonder if he's ever even worn sweats.

Viola paused for a moment and then laughed. Just the thought of Felix in sweats was ridiculous. When the coffee pot had finally dribbled enough to fill a mug, she snatched it up and hurried to the back of the house.

The sunroom was her pride and joy, yet also her chamber of despair. While she loved the wrap around windows, whitewashed floorboards, and exposed brick walls, she had spent many hours sitting in there, staring at her canvases. She'd set them up in a semi-circle surrounding her stool so she could easily move from one to another. In theory, that should have made things easier. In reality, she felt caged in by failure, yet she couldn't get herself to move any of them.

The thought of focusing on one canvas alone was terrifying. If she could just work slowly on all of them at once, it wasn't like she needed to finish any of them soon. It took a long time to complete twelve works of art. As opposed to focusing on one, which would mean she'd need to actually finish it.

Finish it.

Finish it.

The coffee in her mug sloshed onto the floor as she shuddered. Glancing around like someone may be there to judge, she slowly slid her sock over the spill. No point in wasting a towel, right? She fell onto her stool with a sigh, her back to her work. She closed her eyes and chugged the remainder of her coffee.

I just need inspiration. That shouldn't be so hard.

Then why's it so hard?

Her phone, which wasn't allowed in the art studio because it was a distraction, rang from the kitchen counter. Maybe she needed a little distraction? She was across the room and in the kitchen before her ringer could complete it's second round of 'Ice, Ice, Baby,' which happened to be Felix's ringtone.

Oh...No.

She picked up the phone, trying to decide whether to answer or not. If she hadn't ignored his call last week, she'd totally ignore his call today. But two ignored calls in a row would make for a very, very unpleasant third call. After a deep breath, she answered.

"Felix. Hey. Nice to hear from you."

"I'm sure it is, darling. So nice you didn't return my call last week?"

"I'm sorry, I've been so busy painting I've hardly looked at my phone."

"Really? So, you'll have something to show soon?"

"Really soon, Felix."

"I'm glad to hear that, Viola. Very glad." He paused for a moment. "I was preparing for this to be our final conversation."

"Final? You mean..."

"It's been two years, sweetheart. I don't hold on to most clients that long with nothing to show for it."

"I know, Felix. I'm really sorry. I've just struggled with-"

"It doesn't matter now, dear. Because you're moving forward. Besides, it's my job to, how do they say, *pour te donner mon temps*."

"Um. My French is pretty rusty."

"Donner...to give, my dear. It's my job to give you my time." He sighed heavily. "What you choose to do with that time is your choice. Use it to build a thriving art career or squander it in some tiny Tennessee town."

She could just picture him sitting at his massive, antique desk in his downtown office. Feet propped on his footrest while he inspected his perfectly manicured hands. She wiped a sweaty palm down her thigh.

"Right." She was honestly impressed he remembered that it was in Tennessee.

"We'll be talking again real soon, Viola. On video. So I can see this work of yours."

"Oh, I could just text some pictures when it's more finished," she sputtered, waving a dismissive hand. "I don't want to take up your valuable time."

"It is valuable, my dear. And I have a few buyers who have still been asking after you, which is the only reason you and I still have these weekly meetings. So, let's try to keep them happy, hm?"

"Right. You're right, Felix. Thank you."

"Ok, sweetheart. See you real soon. *Au revior*."

Viola held the phone to her ear, even though Felix had already hung up. That was the call she'd been dreading. Well, the prelude to call she was dreading. Being dropped by Felix wasn't an unheard-of thing in the art world, but it definitely wouldn't help her career path. She tried to concentrate on her breathing, but the world felt like it was spinning out from beneath her.

She could feel sweat running down her back as her heart raced in her chest. Pulling in air became difficult as she stood frozen, her mind racing as fast as her heart. She didn't hear when someone walked into her house and barely registered when they steered her towards the kitchen table.

"Viola? Viola?"

Fingers snapped in front of her eyes.

"Come on, girlie. Deep breaths."

When Viola was finally able to relax, she registered that her mentor, Mrs. Bell, was there, patting her hand at the kitchen table, her phone still clenched in the other. Mrs. Bell slid a glass of water across the table towards her.

"Mrs. Bell." Viola took a drink to moisten her dry throat. "Thank you."

"You had me scared there." She held up her own phone and showed Viola the screen. "I was googling symptoms of strokes and aneurisms. Then I stumbled across panic attacks and guessed that was it. I'm no doctor though. We can still call 9-1-1. How's your head? Seeing double?"

Mrs. Bell leaned close and held up three fingers. She then felt Viola's forehead with the back of her hand.

"I'm ok. I think. I'm sorry."

"Don't you apologize to me." Mrs. Bell looked down and shook her head. "There is no shame in feeling your feelings."

"I just meant for scaring you." Viola wrung her hands in her lap.

"How I react is on me, girlie." Mrs. Bell held out a hand and Viola slid hers into it. "Do you want to talk about it?"

"Felix called."

"Ah."

"He said if I don't produce something soon, he'll drop me."

"And that's bad?"

"Of course, that's bad," Viola sputtered. "I owe him my career."

"No." Mrs. Bell shook her head vigorously. "No. He helped sell your pieces. You did the work. He just took his cut. You owe him nothing."

"You don't understand." Viola regretted the words as soon as they left her lips.

"You're right. I never got my big break. But I've also never been driven to a panic attack or driven myself half mad over a project either."

"I just need to find the right inspiration."

Right? That's what I need?

"You need to scrap it all and go for a walk. Get some fresh air. Unpack some boxes and get settled. Go out for dinner. Put up some Christmas decorations." Mrs. Bell stood and threw her hands in the air. "You need to live. That's where you get the inspiration."

"I don't have time." Viola also stood and headed towards her art studio. "I just need to finish these pieces. Then I can do all that."

"Vi, you can't keep going like this." Mrs. Bell followed her. "I'm worried about you."

"Thank you, but, really, I'm ok."

"Baby girl, the saying 'tortured artist' is just that. A saying. Not a reality. Art is supposed to be feeling and passion. This is obsession. It's not healthy."

Viola rubbed at her forehead. They'd had this same conversation a week after she'd moved in.

"Mrs. Bell. I love you. I respect you. But right now, I just need you to support me. Please."

Mrs. Bell stepped around her and stood in front of her semi-circle of canvases. She stood there, saying nothing. It felt like minutes ticked by before she turned back to Viola.

"If support is what you need, then you have it." She turned back to the first painting and swept a finger up the canvas following a splash of red. "This here. This pulls at me. It says something, but the background is muddy. Have you thought about going over it with some oils?"

"I've debated, but Felix said he prefers watercolor purists."

"Well, Felix is a moron." Mrs. Bell bristled, raising up to her full height of five foot nothing. "Adding some oil here and here would bring back the crispness the background needs."

"Ok. I'll think about it."

"Good." Mrs. Bell walked over and put a hand on Viola's elbow. "You sure you're ok?"

"Yes." Viola uncrossed her arms and smiled. "Thank you for checking on me."

"Oh, that reminds me. I brought a casserole." She hurried back to the kitchen and Viola followed. "I was doing some Christmas food prep and figured I better bring one by. The offer is still open to join us for Christmas dinner, you know."

"I know."

"Ok. My Cody will be there."

"Mrs. Bell. For the hundredth time, I am not dating your son." Viola laughed.

"I don't blame you. He's a lazy boy." Mrs. Bell waved a hand at her, causing her to laugh even harder. "But I'm his mother and I love him. And he'd be lucky to end up with a girl like you."

"It's nice to know you still think so." Viola leaned a hip against the kitchen counter.

"Of course, I do. A phase of life doesn't define a person. You'll get through this, and you'll learn the lesson you were meant to." Mrs. Bell pulled her coat off the back of the kitchen chair and put it on. "Just remember what I said about finding that inspiration. Unpack a box or something."

"Will do." Viola leaned down and gave Mrs. Bell a peck on the cheek as she headed for the door.

"And eat something." She hollered over her shoulder before the door closed behind her.

Maybe she's right. Maybe making lunch will spark something.

And spark something it did. A small toaster oven fire to be exact. The cardboard under the frozen pizza wasn't supposed to be included, but she'd been distracted with thinking about possible plans for the afternoon when she tossed it in. So, the house was filled with a lovely burnt paper and pizza smell. Instead of a warm slice for lunch, she ended up gulping down a cup of yogurt and shivering next to an open window to air out the small kitchen.

Unpack a box, she said. I can do that. Just one box.

She picked the top box off the closest stack in the living room. Praying for the universe to put the inspiration she needed in the box, she cut through the tape. Her heart instantly fell when she realized this was the box her mother had dropped off before they headed out of town to visit family. It was full of old childhood mementos, which she highly doubted would contain inspiration for high concept art.

Viola laid down on the floor next to the box, reaching in and grabbing stuff without looking. Each time, she said a small prayer and each time her hopes were dashed. She pulled out an old sociology notebook, a bag stuffed with notes she'd passed with her friends during class, and a friendship bracelet from someone whose name she couldn't even remember from first grade.

"One more chance, Universe." She tossed the friendship bracelet over her shoulder and reached in again. "Show me I'm not forsaken."

Her hand fell on something smooth and hard. A book with bent corners and well-loved pages. The Ugly Duckling had been her favorite story her entire childhood. She'd loved the idea that someone different could grow up to be so admired, special ,and, let's face it, beautiful.

Growing up in the poorest neighborhood in Reverence Ridge meant that she got teased a lot for her hand-me-down clothes that never fit quite right. Her family never had money for her to be in any clubs or sports, and she never found her place with the other kids until she took Mrs. Bell's art class her freshman year of high school. That class changed her life.

So, just like that little ugly duckling, she'd hoped to return home as the polished and poised swan. Instead, she felt like she was just paddling and paddling and getting nowhere, forever stuck in a group of other churning ducklings and never rising above.

She set the book back in the box and closed the flaps, feeling abandoned by the universe. Memory lane wasn't a road she liked to travel often. It left her feeling underachieved and depressed. But it also left her feeling, not necessarily inspired, but driven.

Her canvases sat where she'd left them. She had tried too many inspirations and themes for this collection, and they all stared back at her. One contained her attempt at capturing the night sky, which ended up just looking like black with white speckles. One contained her attempt to show her anxiety, and it looked like...well? It looked like poo. A massive swirl of all colors that turned to a soupy brown in the center. The first piece that Mrs. Bell pointed out with the splash of red was Viola's anger at the rest of the canvas disasters. Anger was an emotion, so Mrs. Bell was right that it felt like something.

Viola sat down in front of that one and picked up her brush. She wet it in her clean water cup and held it over her paint palette. How should she lighten the background? How to make it crisper? Watercolors were used for their beautiful blending and bleeding abilities, not their defined details. Viola tapped her chin with the end of her brush, debating about adding oils. It wasn't something she'd done before and that made her nervous.

Better to stick with what I know. Learning a new technique this late in the game would just add more time.

With her mind made up, she dipped her brush into the red and was holding it above her canvas when her phone rang. Ice, Ice, Baby again.

He couldn't have meant this soon. Could he?

Her hand hovered over her phone as it vibrated on the kitchen counter while she debated. If she didn't answer so soon after talking to him, he'd know she was avoiding him. And she knew what that would lead to- no more agent.

'Felix is a moron.' Mrs. Bell's voice ran through her mind providing her with the ounce of courage she needed to snatch up the phone at the last second and answer.

"Felix. I wasn't expecting to hear from you again today."

"I did say you'd be hearing from me real soon." His voice was short, all business. "I have someone here who's a big fan of yours. You remember Mr. and Mrs. Quandt who purchased several pieces from your last collection?"

"Of course, yes." Viola nibbled on her nails, which were already chewed to nubs.

"Wonderful. Clicking over to video."

What? Viola's head flipped from side to side as she looked for a presentable backdrop for a video call. She raced to her art studio and stood in front of the exposed brick wall. The phone beeped several times, waiting for her to switch over. Looking in the screen, she grimaced when her image appeared. She raked fingers through her hair, but her outfit was a lost cause. Felix would probably drop her on that alone.

She clicked over to video and smiled.

"Ah, there you are." Felix's face took over her screen.

His honey blonde hair was swooped to one side and gelled to perfection. The healthy tan of his skin made his teeth look even whiter. Basically, he was the picture of what you'd expect to find on the front of every golfing magazine. Down to the sockless loafered feet she couldn't see but knew were there.

"Hey, Felix. Long time, no see."

"Well ,that's what happens when you uproot yourself and move across the country, darling."

"Home was calling, what can I say?"

"Hm. Well, as I said, Mr. Quandt is here"

"Oh." Viola's eyes went wide. "He's there? Like there, there?"

"Yes, Viola." Felix huffed out a laugh and looked off screen. "As I said. He's very interested in seeing what you've been working on for so long."

Oh, dear Lord. Not this. Not today. Not right as I'm starting to get a grasp on this painting.

"I don't have anything finished, Felix. Nothing is show worthy at this point." Viola tried to sound firm, but it sounded more like a whine.

"We are both aware of that. He'd just like to see if the current collection will tie in with the previous and find a place in his home."

"Um. It's not like the previous pieces. I went in a different, um, darker direction this time."

"That's just fine." Felix's camera jostled and an older man's face appeared. "I need something a little more...upscale and modern for our home in London."

"Hello, Mr. Quandt. How are you and Mrs. Quandt doing?"

"Just fine. We loved the color and movement in your last pieces. But something darker will suit us just fine."

"Ok..." Viola's voice wavered as she tried to decide what to do.

"Show us the piece that is furthest along, Viola." Felix's said off camera.

"It's really not ready..."

"We understand."

"Alright."

Her feet moved towards the canvas with the splash of red without her giving them the command to do so. The phone trembled in her hand for a moment, but then stilled. She felt terror, disappointment, dread, but also a sense of peace. Like a long-awaited moment had finally arrived.

Her own intake of air was the only thing she heard when she turned the camera to show her canvas. She could still see the screen and saw Mr. Quandt's face look puzzled, then something akin to disgust before he handed the phone to Felix.

"I know the background is muddy. I'm debating touching it up with some oils to add some crispness." Her voice sounded far off, like a faint echo in her ears.

So, this is what an out of body experience feels like.

"And like I said, I'm trying something a little darker, like tapping into anxiety and..."

What was the point of explaining? Two powerful men on the other side of the country couldn't understand where she was coming from. Heck, she didn't even know where she was coming from.

Felix's face filled the screen. His lips were pursed tightly, pulling at the skin below his eyes and creating wrinkles that weren't normally visible.

"Thank you for your time, Viola."

His voice was in sharp focus, snapping her out of her daze. The world suddenly jolted back to life around her. The furnace rumbled. The left-over smell of smoke from lunch. A car raced past the front door. It all came back to her in an instant.

"Please check your email as you'll be receiving correspondence from me. Best of luck with your work."

"Thank you, Fe—"

The call ended.

She knew what an email from Felix meant. He sent them for two reasons. To sign a contract of representation. And to cancel one.

She'd been avoiding this moment for two years, actually much longer. Failure was always just behind her, snapping at her heels like a rabid dog. She kept running, but it was inevitable that it would catch up with her eventually. Today was that day.

She moved toward the wall and pressed her back to it. Deep, aching sobs shook her body as she slid down. Would she ever be enough? Would her work be good enough? Hot tears etched theirs paths down her cheeks. She sat that way and cried until her tears ran dry, but the tightness in her chest remained.

Just like that morning, she slid over to lay down, but remembered to not press her cheek to the floor. Her situation suddenly became very clear to her, and she recognized the ridiculousness. She was laying on the floor in a house she'd rented, but hadn't actually moved into, in a town she hadn't lived in for a decade, crying over losing an agent she never liked in the first place. Her sobs turned to chuckles, which turned to laughter. She curled into a ball, laughing until her stomach hurt.

"Mrs. Bell was right, Felix. You are a moron." Her throat was dry, her voice horse, but she didn't care. "You hear me?"

She pushed herself up and rushed out the back door. The cold evening air bit at her exposed skin and she relished the feeling. The sky was turning into a brilliant, deep blue. Viola jumped down the three steps to her small yard. The ground was freezing, even through her thick socks. Laughter bubbled up again and she threw out her arms and spun, taking in the colors around her for the first time in ages.

"I don't need you," she hollered. "I don't need you, Felix Winfield. I'm better off on my own."

"You tell him, girl." A young woman walked by on the sidewalk bordering her property. She smiled and pumped her fist in the air.

"Yes. Thank you." Viola beamed and pointed at her with both hands.

She took a deep breath, as deep as she could and then rushed inside. A desire to rid herself of the weight of the past two years filled her. The canvases in the semi-circle no longer looked like a cage. She was free of the power they held over her. That Felix held over her. She grabbed up three of the paintings and stomped to the kitchen for a garbage bag.

"No more." She looked at each one, finally seeing it for what they really were. Shackles. Leaches. Disasters. Then she waggled her fingers in a wave as she dropped each of them into the trash. "No. More."

Back in the art studio, she looked at the canvas with the splash of red with fresh eyes. She started laughing again. No wonder Mr. Quandt and Felix looked disgusted. It looked like a smeared tomato on rotten lettuce. That one went in the trash next. She worked her way down the line until she came to the poo painting. For some reason, she just couldn't part with it.

"I'll learn the lesson I'm supposed to learn." Viola repeated Mrs. Bell's words from that morning. "I think you, dear poo painting, will be the perfect reminder."

With the manic determination only a newly learned life lesson can provide, she stormed into the living room and propped the canvas up on the mantle. Her hammer was packed in a box somewhere, so hanging it would have to wait. But it seemed fitting that this would be the first decoration hung in the new house.

"So I never forget."

Out of the corner of her eye, she noticed a gift bag sitting by the front door that she knew wasn't something of hers. Mrs. Bell must have left it as a surprise. Viola had to think about what day it even was. Only three days left until Christmas, and she didn't have a single decoration up. In Reverence Ridge that was not acceptable. It was surprising no one had snuck a wreath up on her door or offered to hang some lights for her.

She reached for the giftbag, feeling guilty for her grinchiness. Inside the tissue paper, Viola found a miniature sculpting set. Tiny chisels, hammers, files, and brushes in all different shapes. There were also blocks of different rocks, wood, and hardened clay. A note lay at the bottom.

"Viola,

Merry Christmas! Maybe trying something different will knock some ideas loose.

Love, Mrs. Bell"

Viola had never sculpted in her life. She was about to set the bag down when a pure white rock rolled out of the corner. It was rough in her hand but sparkled like a ball of ice. She stared at it, the shape of it. It's edges and planes. Something began forming in her mind, and she grabbed the little tool kit and ran to the art studio. Her hands trembled as she held the chisel to the surface, but for the first time in too long, it was from excitement and not nerves.

Her first tap of the hammer to the chisel sent a thrill through her. The second strike was no less exciting. Over, and over, and over, she chipped into the stone. She played with the different shapes of chisels and files, discovering ways to get what she wanted. In her flurry of inspiration, a coating of white dust, glistening like snow, spread across her worktable.

Finally, she held the finished product in her palm. It was a little rough around the edges, but for once Viola wasn't focusing on the mistakes. What she saw was possibility. Viola pulled out her phone and shot off a quick text to Mrs. Bell.

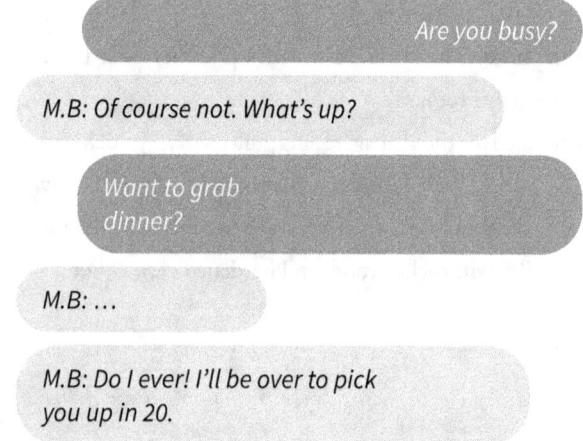

Are you busy?

M.B: Of course not. What's up?

Want to grab dinner?

M.B: ...

M.B: Do I ever! I'll be over to pick you up in 20.

Viola took a few minutes to attach a hanging string to her little sculpture and wrap it back up in the gift bag Mrs. Bell had left her. Then she hurried to her room to change. She had to dig pretty deep in the drawers to find anything that wasn't sweatpants, but finally she found some nice tan slacks and dark gray halter top. With a creamy cardigan and blingy necklace, she felt like a new woman.

When the doorbell rang, she was just dabbing on some lip gloss. She pulled open the door with a flourish and waved Mrs. Bell inside.

"Well," her mentor laughed. "This is quite the change since this morning."

"Sometimes change is necessary." Viola threaded her hand through Mrs. Bell's arm and lead her to the living room.

"Couldn't agree more, my girl." Mrs. Bell smiled warmly; her age only betrayed by the smile lines at the corner of her eyes. "So, what kind of change are we talking here?"

"Big ones." Viola propped a hip on the arm of the sofa. "Felix dropped me."

"Oh, Viola, I'm so sorry. I know how important his help and guidance were to you."

"Don't be sorry. You were right. About it all," Viola huffed. "Felix is a moron."

"Thank God." Mrs. Bell clasped her chest dramatically and fell onto the sofa beside Viola. "I'm so glad you finally realized that. I was getting to the end of my tolerance with that one."

"Yep. It's time to move on. In a lot of ways." Viola grabbed the gift bag and set it in Mrs. Bell's lap. "For you."

"This was for you. I won't take it back. You're talking about change, and this could be good for you."

"Just open the bag." Viola laughed and stood up to find the box she'd dug through earlier that day.

"Oh," Mrs. Bell gasped. "Viola, this is lovely. You did this in one afternoon? I knew you'd take to sculpting."

Viola wiggled onto the seat next to her. In her palm sat the swan Viola had carved, it's wings and neck outstretched.

"The movement in this piece is stunning." Mrs. Bell turned it, inspecting it from every angle. "It looks like it could take off from my hand at any moment. Or like its dancing. Whatever it's doing, it looks joyous."

"Joy and freedom." The corner of Viola's mouth raised slightly. "I don't know if I ever told you how much your class meant to me in high school. I was too embarrassed. But your class changed my life."

Viola placed The Ugly Duckling book on her lap and ran a finger over the aged cover. The plastic coating was peeling, and the color was faded.

"I always felt like this duckling, well, gosling. I never fit in anywhere until I discovered art. You gave my life meaning and all the things you say art is—passion, emotion, desire. But most of all, you gave me a home. That art room was my safe space when everywhere else felt so volatile."

Mrs. Bell turned to fully face her, tucking a foot up under her other leg. "Viola, I had no idea. I mean, I knew things weren't great for you, but I didn't know they were that bad."

"I'd hoped that, with Felix's help, I'd finally be that swan. Finally fit in and reach my full potential, like leveling up. But I got the exact opposite. He always made me feel like I wasn't good enough and needed to be...more. But not you. The only thing you've ever pressured me to be is happy.

I asked the universe today to provide me inspiration, and it led me to this book. I didn't see it at first, but when I opened myself up to it, the emotion jumped right out. I know this swan isn't perfect, but I wanted you to know what it meant to me. What you mean to me."

Mrs. Bell wiped at the corners of her eyes before pulling her in for a hug. When she pulled back, she was staring at something on the opposite wall.

"I will cherish it always, but I have to ask," she pointed to the mantel. "Is that staying there?"

"The poo painting?"

"Is that it's official name?" Mrs. Bell raised an eyebrow.

"Yep." Viola answered with no hesitation. "A reminder of the lesson learned."

"I mean, that's great. But... right in the living room?"

"Ok, well, once I actually unpack it may move somewhere else, but I kind of like it there." They both rose from the couch, and Viola ushered Mrs. Bell towards the door. "So, how about that dinner? Or would you like to continue critiquing my life choices?"

"Oh, I think we can manage both at the same time, don't you? May as well do it with food."

"Ha, ok." Viola tugged on her coat and followed Mrs. Bell out into the night.

"So, is this a consolatory dinner after what Mr. Felix did to you?" Mrs. Bell pulled out her keys and walked around to the driver's side of her little VW Bug. "Will alcohol and ice cream be required?"

"Nope. This is a celebratory dinner. My options have finally opened up. I feel...hopeful." Viola thought for a moment. "But alcohol and ice cream can definitely still be involved."

Celia

C elia rubbed a dab of cold cream into her palm. On their date last night, Walt had commented on how soft her hand felt in his. Now, she knew she would need to keep up her moisturizing routine. Besides, rubbing in the lotion helped ease the ache in her stiff fingers.

Her phone buzzed on the table next to her recliner. She reached for it, grasping the edges so she wouldn't smear lotion on the screen. Squinting, she tapped it and held it to her ear.

"Hello?"

Celia jumped when the phone continued to ring in her ear. She muttered and pressed at the screen again.

"Hello?"

"Hey, mom."

"Oh, Sarah. How are you?" Celia squinted at the screen again, trying to remember which button turned on speaker phone. She tapped one, hoping for the best. When her daughter's voice changed over, she sighed and set the phone down on her TV tray.

"I'm good." Sarah said. "How are you this morning?"

"Oh, my fingers are pretty stiff. It's this cold front coming through, I'm sure."

"Sorry about your fingers, Mom. But how was your date with Mr. Palmer? I'm dying to know. I thought you were going to call last night."

"Oh, I got in pretty late." Celia smiled at the memory. "I knew you'd be putting Pax to bed, so I didn't want to interrupt."

"Seriously? I would have fed him sugar straight out the bag and let him stay up all night so I could hear about your date. It's all you've talked about this week."

"You're so sweet, thinking about your ol' mother."

Celia snuggled further down into her recliner, the leather aged and soft. Her Christmas tree sat in the corner, blinking merrily, and she couldn't help but to feel wrapped in comfort.

"Mom! Spill the beans already."

"Ok. Ok." Celia chuckled and dabbed more cold cream on the other hand. "It was a wonderful evening. We went to the diner, you know? He opened the door for me and took my coat. Such a gentleman, that Walt."

"Aw. That's so sweet." Sarah sighed. "What did you guys talk about?"

"Oh, you know us old folks. We talked about our ailments, what medications we're taking. Oh, he mentioned he preferred turkey to ham sandwiches for lunch."

"Oh. Well, that sounds nice."

"Seriously, Sarah? We may be in our seventies, but that doesn't mean we have nothing to talk about anymore. Medications and ailments. Oh brother."

"Well, someone's full of spit and vinegar this morning. I take it the date went well then?"

"Yes. It really did."

"That's great, Mom. I'm really happy for you." Sarah covered the phone and yelled something about getting ready to Pax. "Will you be going out again?"

"We didn't arrange anything, but I sure hope so."

"Are you just going to sit around and wait for him to ask or what? Take charge. Ask him."

"Oh, I don't know about that."

"It's the twenty-first century, Mom. Feminism, equal rights and all that." She hollered to someone in the background again then sighed. "Pax is worried Santa won't be able to find him at your place tomorrow night."

"Oh dear." Celia thought a moment. "Tell him I sent a letter to Santa to make sure he knew Pax would be at my house."

The clock on the wall dinged 8 o'clock. She'd been up and had a nice calm breakfast already, but she knew this time of morning was a real scramble for her daughter.

"Perfect. Thank you. Listen, I gotta go. He is not getting ready for school, and we are going to be so, so late."

"Ok, honey. Give him a kiss from Nana. Can't wait to see you tomorrow."

"Will do. We can't wait either. Love you."

"Love you."

Celia could hear Sarah hollering as she clicked off the phone. That stage of life was so busy, all the time. She leaned back in her chair enjoying the silence of her own little house. Then her phone dinged again. It was a text from Sarah.

> S: Ask him out.

Celia pecked at her phone with the tip of her pinkie, still worried about lotion onher screen.

> I'll think about it.

> S: What have you got to lose?

> S: If Walt can't handle a strongwoman, he doesn't deserve you.

> S:<3 <3 <3

Celia fanned her hands in front of her to help the lotion dry and thought about what Sarah had said. What did she really have to lose? If something that small could scare off Walt, then good riddance. Well, maybe that was a little harsh. There weren't that many eligible men in her dating pool. Reverence Ridge had a lot of wonderful qualities, but an abundance of mature, single men was not one of them. Especially not ones with a lush, full head of hair like Walt still had.

"Daggumit. I'm going for it." Celia pushed herself out of her recliner and started towards the door, but then veered towards the kitchen. "Better not arrive empty handed."

In the kitchen, Celia eyed the chocolate mousse pie she'd made for her book club meeting the next day. There would be plenty of time to make another, and she distinctly remembered Walt saying how much he liked chocolate. This pie had won her first place at the summer fair five years running, beating out that obnoxious Wini from down the street. With that decided, Celia headed to her bedroom to freshen up.

It was supposed to be extra cold and windy, so Celia chose her heaviest long skirt and a warm, blue sweater. Sarah said the color accentuated her gray eyes. Not that Walt would see her sweater under her coat. Unless he invited her in. And she really hoped he would. She brushed at the soft waves in her hair. Gray was officially the majority over the light auburn it used to be. She was torn about dying it. Sarah had recently told her she pulled off the gray well. Apparently, it also went with her eyes. Part of her missed the fiery redhead she'd been for so long, but, turning side to side in the mirror, she decided she could totally pull off the gray. With a grin at her reflection, she flipped off the light and set out to surprise Walt.

The wind whipped at her as soon as she set foot outside. It bit right through her coat and swirled around her ankles. The nice waves she'd worked for in her hair were gone instantly, replaced by a rippling mass of tentacles, sticking to her lips, covering her eyes, and doing everything but staying in place. Balancing the pie in one hand while the wind blew was going to result in a sidewalk covered in award winning chocolate mousse. So, she clamped both hands on the edges of the pie pan and resigned to fix her hair on Walt's porch before ringing the bell.

At the end of her walk, she turned back to quickly close the gate. When she turned back around, a shock of bright red caught her eye. Another woman several houses down had just stepped onto the sidewalk. Celia paused and her eyes narrowed.

The other woman paused too, staring at Celia. A tray of cookies rested in her hands. Her eyes darted to Walt's porch as her red ankle-length coat billowed around her like the petals of an oleander. Lovely from a distance, but toxic up close. Just like Celia's neighbor.

The two women stared while wind whipped around them, but the other woman made the first move, rushing off the curb. Celia was only a step behind when they met in the middle of the street. Neither looked at the other, just continued walking quickly towards Walt's house.

"Celia." The woman's voice dripped with false sincerity.

"Wini," Celia said curtly. "What brings you out today?"

"Same as you I suppose." Wini flicked her eyes to Celia's pie and sniffed.

Celia reached Walt's front gate first and pulled it open just far enough for herself. Wini wedged herself in next to her, pushing her hip against Celia's a little rougher than necessary. Celia stumbled a step, clutching her pie. She growled and spat her hair out of her mouth as Wini rushed up the front steps and rang the bell before her.

"We missed you at book club last week." Celia hurriedly ran fingers through her hair with one hand, holding onto the pie with the other.

"Did you really?" The fake sincerity was back, overly sweet.

"No. Not really."

"Well," Wini bristled, "some of us have better things todo than sit around gabbing."

"Oh, like what?" Celia squared her shoulder's to Wini's. "Getting tacky dye jobs at the salon?"

"Better to look fake and fresh than old and drab, Celia. Besides, did you even manage to brush that gray mess this morning?"

The comeback Celia had was cut off when the door opened, and Walt smiled at them both.

"Ladies, what are you two talking about out here?"

"Oh, just discussing Celia's awful case of bedhead today. Poor dear." Wini tsked her tongue and looked at Celia with concern.

"Meh, happens to the best of us." Walt winked at her. "The sign of a good night's sleep and a clean conscience my mom used to say."

Celia grinned at him, patting her windblown tresses back into place. Walt wore a brown button-down shirt, unbuttoned, with a white t-shirt beneath, and a nicely pressed pair of khakis. Celia knew Walt would never wear something that nice just to sit around the house.

"I don't want to keep you from your plans, Walt." Celia edged herself inside the screen door in front of Wini. "I just wanted to bring this over and let you know that I had a really wonderful time last night."

Her grin widened when she felt Wini stiffen next to her.

"Is this one of your famous chocolate mousse pies?" Walt licked his lips. "I've been dying to try one of these. People rave about them."

"Well," Celia raised her shoulders bashfully and handed him the pie, "I thought it was about time you tried one."

"I'm surprised you haven't had any yet, Walt. I thought everyone would have tried some by now with how often Celia makes them." Wini edged a step in front of Celia with her plate of cookies. "Now that I think about it, I've never seen you make anything else. But I mean, not everyone can be a wiz in the kitchen. If you find something that works for you, go with it."

"I can't wait to try a piece." Walt lifted the pie pan towards Celia. "Thanks, Ceel."

"Oh, yes. Here. Why don't you try one of my cookies?" Wini reached under the plastic wrap and pulled out a cookie. She held it up to Walt's mouth.

"Thanks. I just finished breakfas— "

"Oh, just one little bite." She wiggled the cookie in front of his lips. "Why wait?"

"I'm ok. Oh, um. Ok then."

Wini coaxed the cookie into his mouth as he was talking. He nibbled a small bite, wiping the crumbs from his lips.

"Mmmm. Very tasty. Thanks for that."

"My pleasure. I baked these just for you." Wini passed the plate to him and patted his hand as he took it. "And I just wanted to say that I'm really looking forward to our lunch this afternoon."

Celia's stomach dropped. A lunch date? Was that why he was dressed up? Wini turned to her with a smug smile and stepped back.

"While I'd love to invite you both in for pie, cookies, and coffee, but I've got an appointment with my barber."

"Oh, that's ok. I'll be seeing you shortly anyway." Wini beamed.

"Yes." Walt pointed the cookie plate towards her in place of his hand. "And Celia, I had a great time last night, too. Thank you for the pie."

"You're very welcome. Now we'll get out of your hair. Wouldn't want to keep you from your barber." Celia chuckled at her own joke.

"Are you implying there's something wrong with Walt's hair?" Wini crossed her arms and raised a brow in Celia's direction. "I think those lush locks of yours look perfect, Walt. Don't let anyone tell you any different."

Celia's cheeks burned with embarrassment and rage. How was she able to take every single thing people said and turn it into an insult? God blessed her abundantly in that department. Celia couldn't see a use for such a skill outside alienating everyone. And who would want that?

They both waved, and Walt closed the door slowly, balancing both pie and cookies in one arm. Then, they both turned on their heels and stalked down the porch steps and out the front gate. Before they split off in the middle of the road, they shared a heated glare and stomped towards their houses.

"Oh, Celia, dear," Wini called from her walk. "I'll send you my stylist's name. She could do wonders for those tangles of yours."

"Oh, go break a hip." Celia muttered as she yanked her door open.

She quickly glanced back at Walt's house. It was a charming two-story craftsman, just like all the homes on their block. But what his lacked was holiday cheer.

"Not even a wreath on the door, Walt?" Celia shook her head as she walked inside. "Hey, there's an idea."

There was no way she'd let Wini snatch him away from her right as they were finally getting to know each other. Maybe the pie wasn't enough. She needed to step up her game. Rubbing her hands together, both for warmth and due to a plan forming, she decided to head into town for some wreath making supplies.

> Is it too needy to make a man a pie and a wreath the day after a first date?

S: That's pretty thirsty, Mom.

S: What are you doing?

> So that's a yes?

S: Typically, I'd say yes. But maybe geriatric dating is different.

S:...

Don't even say it.

S: Maybe you can move quicker because you don't have as much time.

I said don't.

Listen to your mother.

S: You asked.

S: My opinion- Do whatever floats your boat. Enjoy your golden years.

Celia rolled her eyes. But Sarah did have a point. They weren't getting any younger. Who cared if she was being needy or thirsty? What did that even mean? She decided she didn't have time to decode current lingo and grabbed her car keys.

The drive to the town square was quick. Even on the busiest day of the Christmas season, to get from the two furthest points in town wouldn't take much more than twenty minutes. It made Celia's heart swell with pride and appreciation to see all the cars parked outside the shops. She pulled into the parking lot for Tin Soldier General and parked as close as possible.

"Hey, Carol." Celia waved at the woman behind the cash register on her way to the back of the store.

The wire wreath frames and deco mesh were heaped on a shelf at the back. Wreath making was always a popular hobby in Reverence Ridge due to the town's love of Christmas, so the supplies were kept well stocked year-round. But with it being the day before Christmas Eve, everything was pretty picked over. Celia's options were a dark navy that had droplets of something red on it, a putrid green, hot pink, and silver. She snatched up the silver instantly, then debated between the vile green and the spilled-on-navy.

Her hand hovered over the green. "Oh, what am I thinking? That would look like a wreath of snot. I'd never hear the end of it from Wini."

She grabbed the navy and headed towards the counter.

"Hey, Celia. Making more wreaths?" Carol asked as she rang up the items.

"Just one for my neighbor. His door is, sadly, bare."

"That's so thoughtful of you."

"According to Sarah, that's very thirsty of me."

"What in the world does that mean?"

"You got me." Celia shrugged. "I can't keep up with the lingo anymore."

"I gave up trying after 'sup?' and 'da bomb' with my own kids." Carol sighed and waved, moving on to the next customer in line.

As Celia loaded the supplies into the trunk, she decided to stop on the square to see if she could find any decorations for the wreath. The bookstore always had little knick-knacks that would be fun to add some personality. She drove over a block and parked as close to MistleTomes as she could.

As she walked past the diner, she glanced in and stopped in her tracks. Sitting at a table by the front windows were Walt and Wini eating lunch. As she watched, Wini tossed her black hair over her shoulder and laughed at something Walt said.

"Ugh, please." Celia rolled her eyes.

Walking towards the bookstore, she focused all her anger and annoyance on Wini. She knew if she let that go, the only thing left behind was the pain and betrayal from Walt. She couldn't believe he was out with another woman so soon after their first date. And why of all women, Winifred Taylor?

Celia squared her shoulders and marched into MistleTomes. Muttering under her breath and using the word 'hussie' far too often, she stormed to the back aisles where cute, little decorations and ornaments were sold. For a few minutes, she pawed through the shelves without actually seeing what she was looking at. Visions of Walt and Wini kept dancing through her head.

"Ugh. Even their names go together," Celia whispered, curling her top lip in frustration.

She spun around to look at the other side of the aisle, scooting boxes from side to side without paying any attention to what was inside them.

Hadn't they had a charming evening, sharing stories of their lives, and splitting a cherry cheesecake, not because they were hungry, but because they didn't want the night to end? Had she just been reading into things? A case of wishful thinking?

Or, maybe, Walt was a plier, or whatever Sarah called them. A real tool. A ladies' man. A cheater.

"A regular old Casanova," Celia scoffed.

"If you're looking for Casanova, you're in the wrong section."

Celia whipped around, her hand flying to her chest. Skye, the owner of MistleTomes, stood at the end of the aisle, waving awkwardly. Her purple hair was pulled up into a messy bun, held in place with what looked to Celia like chop-sticks.

"Oh, Skye." Celia sighed. "You startled me."

"Sorry, Miss Celia." Skye swayed to the background music as she straightened a few things on the shelves. "You just blew right past me, so I figured you knew what you wanted. But then you were back here for a while, so I thought I'd see if you needed any help."

"I'm sorry, dear."

"It's ok. I was just checking." Skye made a step to leave, but then stepped back and asked hesitantly "Is everything ok?"

"Oh, I'll be fine." Celia huffed then looked at Skye's expectant face. "It's just...boy trouble."

"Ohhh." Skye sagged with relief. "I feel you there, let me tell you."

"Right?" Celia nodded. "You'd think at my age I'd be done with that nonsense, yet here I am again. What is it about those senseless, scatter-brained menfolk? Hm? What is it?"

"They need us, Miss. Celia. That's what." Skye's hands moved to her hips, and she rocked back on her heels. "They'd never survive without us."

"You are so right." Celia laughed. "How'd you get so wise at such a young age?"

"Watched my mom go through men like I go through books, which is," she gestured at the shop around them, "a lot."

"Ah. Well, it takes a wise woman to learn from another's mistakes."

"Well, can't say I haven't made my own. Or won't be making more soon." Skye sagged again, this time in frustration. "But, seriously, what is it with these menfolk?"

"Soon, eh?" Celia stepped closer and lowered her voice. "You've got your eyes set on someone?"

"It's a little early to say anything official, but maybe." Skye's cheeks flushed as her eyes flicked to the ceiling. "And what about you? What dapper gentleman has caught your fancy?"

"Just a neighbor of mine."

"Walt." Skye gasped and danced from foot to foot. "Oh, you two would be so adorable together. Like a Lucy and Desi, except, well..."

"Old?" Celia deadpanned.

"Your words." Skye held her palms up in defense.

"We would be cute together, wouldn't we?" Celia smiled. "Cuter than say, Walt and Wini?"

"Winifred? Um, definitely. Walt is way too down-to-earth for her." Skye nodded vigorously. "Walt is front porch rocking chairs and blue jeans. Wini is fine dining and designer dresses. That wouldn't mesh well."

"And what am I?" Celia asked.

"You're chocolate pie and lemonade on a summer's day, Miss Celia. Traditional yet refreshing at the same time."

Celia liked the sound of that. A smile spread across her face, and she reached out to hug Skye. There may have been forty years difference between them, but, right then, there was very little space between their hearts. Some problems were universal, no matter the age. And those pesky menfolk tended to top the list.

"Whoever has caught your eye is a lucky man indeed," Celia whispered before pulling back. "Now, I need to decorate a wreath."

"Oh. Ok then." Skye's hands spun in front of her as she adjusted to the change in conversation. "I've got ornaments and small knick-knacks over here."

Skye pointed towards the next aisle and walked Celia over to the section she'd mentioned. At the sound of the bells on the door, Skye disappeared to the front of the shop, leaving Celia on her own again.

Her hand closed over an ornament of ice skates. Walt had told her that he used to go skating with his brother. Plus, with navy and silver mesh, an ice and skating theme would work perfectly. She quickly grabbed anything else related to ice skating and hurried to the front to check out.

"Find what you needed?" Skye asked as she rang up the items.

"I definitely did." Celia paid and grabbed her bags but stopped before turning towards the door. "Thanks for that heart-to-heart back there."

"Us ladies have got to stick together, right?"

"So right."

Celia left the bookstore feeling lighter than when she'd entered, even though she now carried several bags of decorations. There was no way all of this would fit on one wreath, but she liked to have options. And it wasn't like it wouldn't get used on wreaths next year anyway.

As Celia shifted one bag to her other hand, she wasn't paying attention, and her foot hit the edge of the curb. Since there was snow, she didn't go head over heels, just fell gracefully to the ground in what her grandson would have dubbed 'epic slow-mo.'

"Oh, for the love." She threw her hands up, bags and all, and let them fall back to her sides. Cold wetness began to seep through the back of her skirt, which she knew would be soaked by the time she got up. "At least no one is here to see this."

"Celia? Is that you?"

She turned and looked through her curtain of hair at none other than Wini, with Walt at her side. The smirk on Wini's face let her know that her predicament of being sprawled out in the street was more entertaining than cause for alarm.

"Perfect, just perfect," she muttered.

"Celia, darling, what on earth are you doing down there?" Wini asked.

"Let me help." Walt was at her side, one foot on the sidewalk, another in the street next to her to brace himself as he lifted her from the ground. "Are you alright? Do we need to call Doc?"

"I'm fine. I'm fine." She brushed away his fussing hands. "Just got lost in my thoughts and missed the curb, that's all."

"Are you sure?" Walt's brow was creased with concern. His sandy hair fell over his forehead. "We can get Doc over here in no time."

"That's not necessary. I promise. I'm fine." She reached out and patted his hand. "Thank you for your help though. I'm lucky you came along when you did."

"Well, you should probably hurry home, Ceels," Wini said from the curb. "You're soaking wet. We wouldn't want you to catch a chill. And you look a fright, dear."

Celia closed her eyes and took a deep breath.

"Thank you for your concern, Wini. I think I'll do just that."

"Where are you parked? I can at least walk you." Walt's hand rested on her elbow.

"No. No. I wouldn't want to intrude on your lunch."

"Oh, lunch is over." Walt waved that off.

"But we were heading to Tin Soldier General," Wini pouted.

"Pretty sure that can wait," Walt said.

"I am fine." Celia said over the two of them as they continued to talk. "My car is right there. I'm heading straight home. No big deal."

"You're sure?" Walt looked very uncertain.

"Positive." Celia began walking towards her car, ignoring the squelching of her shoes. "Enjoy the general store."

She waved as Walt stood watching her until Wini tugged at his arm. Celia watched over her shoulder as he slowly turned and walked the opposite direction with Wini draped over his arm. She sighed and dusted off her skirt as best she could with her hands full of bags.

Was all this even worth it? Should a woman of her age even be running after a man? Especially one brazen enough to flaunt another woman in front of her? Celia's shoulders stooped as she shuffled towards her car, wet socks squeaking inside her shoes the whole way.

She tossed the bags into the back seat and cranked the heater up to high. When the seat warmer kicked in, she was glad she'd let Sarah talk her into getting a new car. Some of the more modern conveniences were worth the exorbitant sticker price. And all the cup holders? Added bonus.

Celia plugged her phone into the charger and dialed Sarah's number.

"Hey, Mom. I'm on my lunch-break. What's up?"

Celia could hear her chewing in the background and smiled.

"Another salad today?" She asked over the crunching.

"Of course. That's the only thing this cafeteria can manage to not burn or mangle in some fashion."

Sarah worked as a pediatric RN at the hospital in Gatlinburg. Celia hated her being in another town, but job opportunities of any kind were scarce in the area, especially for something so specialized.

"I'm sorry, honey. We can prep some freezer meals for you when you come down for Christmas."

"I know you didn't call to talk about my lunch options. So, what's up?"

"Well, there has been a bit of a development with Walt."

"Oh really?"

Celia could practically see her daughter leaning into the table, getting comfy, waiting for the juicy details. While Celia didn't usually give gossip much mind, Sarah had a nose for it. She could dig up all the information faster than a truffle pig in a forest.

"Not a good kind, I'm afraid."

"What'd he do? Do I need to come down there and give him a talkin' to?"

"No, no." Celia laughed. "That won't be necessary. Ok?"

"I make no promises where your honor and feelings are concerned, Mom. If he hurt you, he'll answer to me."

She didn't doubt that for an instant. She remembered Sarah's first high school breakup. James Milton. Poor guy didn't know what he'd gotten himself into when he dumped Sarah for one of the cheerleaders. He had a better idea the next morning when he woke up to raw egg, peanut butter, and plastic wrap all over his prized Mustang. Sarah spent that afternoon scrubbing it off as punishment, but she'd done it with a satisfied smirk on her face while James cowered inside the house.

"Promise me we won't have another James Milton incident. It's far too cold this time of year to scrub frozen egg off a windshield."

"No promises." Her voice was serious. "I may be attempting a Blitzen when we get there tomorrow."

"Well, unless you're planning on galloping over on a reindeer, I think the word you want is blitzkrieg."

"Reindeer. I mean, 'tis the season." Sarah paused to take another bite. "So, what'd Gramps do?"

Celia filled Sarah in on all the details of her morning. Delivering the pie. Running into Wini. Their conversation with Walt. Then seeing them at the diner and after falling.

"First of all, I'd be a bad daughter if I didn't ask. Are you ok? You didn't hurt anything when you fell?"

"No. I'm fine."

"Ok. Good." Sarah took a deep breath. "Winifred Taylor? Seriously? Did she know you went out with him?"

"Of course..."

"And she still went to lunch with him?"

"Yep. And this from the woman who just last week at the town meeting told me she preferred bald men. And now here she is going after the only one with a good amount of hair left."

Celia glanced in the rearview mirror, patting at her own hair, and started the drive home. She waved to Pastor Robert as he, and several church staff, were covering the nativity with a tarp. It wouldn't do to have Baby Jesus blowing down the road.

"She probably just wants him because you do." Sarah huffed. "Like a little kid wanting a toy just because someone else has it."

"Well, she is rather immature."

"Pffft. You don't have to tell me." There was more shuffling in the background. Her lunch break was probably almost over. "So, the real question here is what are you going to do about it?"

What should she do? Celia wasn't even sure it was worth the effort to make the wreath anymore. They had a lovely evening together, and less than 24 hours later he's out with Wini? If it was Maggie, or one of the other ladies from church, she could at least understand the appeal, even if it didn't make her happy. Growing old alone was lonely sometimes, but she knew it was better to be alone than with someone she couldn't trust.

"That's why I called you." Celia pulled into her driveway and threw the car into park. "I don't know what to do. What would you do?"

"I think we both know what I'd do." Then she coughed out the words, "Cough. James Milton. Cough."

"I'm far too old to be slathering peanut butter on anyone's door handles, dear. Other suggestions?"

"Mom. What does your heart say? You've been pining over this guy since he moved in two years ago. Are you going to give him up at the first struggle? Let Wini win? Or are you going to fight and show him how damn lucky he'd be to have a woman like you at his side?"

"Well, when you put it that way it doesn't seem like I have much of a choice at all." Celia tilted her head, thinking for a moment, and then began to nod slowly. "You're right. I can't give up at the first bump in the road."

"There's my Mom. Go get him, tiger."

"Thanks, sweetie. Now go help those patients of yours. And don't forget to eat a granola bar or something. We all know what happens when your sugar gets low. And those poor, sick kids don't deserve that."

"Gee, thanks, Mom."

"Anytime. Love you."

After gathering her shopping bags from the back seat, she hurried inside out of the frigid cold. The seat warmer had worked wonders, but her skirt was still damp, and that wind was in a biting mood. Once inside, she hurried to her room to change out of the wet clothes. As soon as she was in a dry pair of slacks and a comfy Christmas sweater, she felt like a new, much warmer, woman.

"Let's see what kind of magic we can work up here." Celia said as she emptied the bags on the table.

Most of the decorations she bought were ornaments, so they would attach easily. A few would need a hot glue gun, which she brought up from the basement, along with a wire wreath frame. She set to work, humming as she wound the mesh fabric around the frame. Luckily, she was able to wipe off and hide most of the sticky red splotches on the navy.

Soon, she was ready to add the ornaments to really make the wreath special. Walt had told her about skating with his brother when they were little, so she picked out an ornament of two little boys on a frozen lake and a couple ice skates. After she got the big decorations attached, she picked out sparkly snowflakes and scattered them throughout the fabric.

Holding it out in front of her, she knew it wasn't her best wreath, but on such short notice, it would have to do. Walt probably wouldn't care about the abundance, or lack thereof, of decorations or their symmetry anyway. After fluffing the bow at the bottom, it was ready for delivery.

She pulled on her coat and headed out the door with the wreath. The sun was starting to set, and the wind had picked up. Celia shivered and pulled her hood on; thankful it hadn't been this cold when she'd slipped earlier. She would have frozen stiff before even making it to her heated seats.

At the end of the front walk, she turned to fight the gate closed. The wind pushed at it something fierce. When it was finally latched, she clamped both hands on the wreath before it tumbled down the road with the next big gust. When she glanced down the road to check for traffic, she saw someone else struggling to close their front gate.

"You again? Seriously?" Celia called out.

"Oh, did you miss me?" Wini scowled in her direction, holding tightly to a loaf of sweet bread.

Both ladies lifted their chins and refused to look at one another as they shuffled across the road. The wind whipped around them, blowing their coats and hair in all directions. Celia clamped a hand down on her hood to hold it in place. Wini's ankle length coat acted like a sail, filling with wind around her legs and pulling her down the street several steps.

They were both out of breath by the time they made it to the other side. Once on Walt's front walk, the house blocked most of the wind, and they were able to stop.

"Banana bread, huh? You actually make that or just repackage a loaf from Tin Soldier?" Celia threw back her hood and smoothed her hair with one hand.

"Well, I don't have to ask if you made that wreath. It has a lovely homemade aesthetic about it." Wini grabbed at her coat, tugging it back where it belonged.

They both narrowed their eyes and turned towards the door with a huff. Wini stepped up the middle of the stairs, not allowing Celia to pass her and rang the bell.

"We had a lovely lunch in case you were wondering." Wini stared at the door, not bothering to turn around. "Glad to see you out of those sopping clothes we saw you in earlier."

The door opened just as Celia growled in response. She wiped the frown from her face and smiled as Walt stepped out. Smiling wasn't hard when he was around.

"Ladies, are we making this a tradition now? Nice to see you both." He smiled at each of them. "Come on it. It's freezing out here tonight."

"Oh, thank you." Wini reached out a hand for Walt to assist her through the door. "I was just telling Celia how glad I am she isn't still in those wet clothes from earlier."

Celia rolled her eyes then planted a smile back on her face as Walt reached out to help her through the door as well.

"Thank you, Walt."

He held her fingers for a moment before moving past her down the hall toward the living room. Wini had already peeled off her coat and thrown it over the back of the couch. She wore a thin red turtleneck with a long black skirt. Celia rubbed her free hand over her slacks, feeling rather frumpy.

"Wini I'm glad you're here." Walt turned towards his kitchen. "I have something for you."

Celia's heart sank as Wini smirked at her behind Walt's back. The wreath dropped to her side, and she took a step back towards the door. Sarah was right; it was the twenty-first century. She *was* a strong woman and deserved someone who respected her. The way Walt was acting was unacceptable. To be so nonchalant about it, too? As Sara would say, 'that was cold. So cold.' Maybe the James Milton threat didn't sound like such a bad idea after all. He returned a few moments later with a stack of papers.

"I was thinking more about the church fundraiser after lunch today and had some ideas. I wrote them out and also printed off all the files from previous fundraisers so we can go through them and see what options were the most profitable."

The church fundraiser? So, their lunch had been a meeting this whole time? Celia lowered her head and chuckled. When she glanced back up, Wini's cheeks were almost the same shade of red she loved to wear.

"Thank you, Walt," Wini said primly, grasping the papers with her fingertips. "I'll go over them once Christmas is over."

"Of course. I also wrote down the prices we saw at Tin Soldier. Wouldn't want to forget and have to make another trip."

"No. We wouldn't want that." Wini pursed her lips and turned towards her coat. "Before I go, here's a loaf of banana bread. A nice little holiday treat, hm?"

"Oh, you didn't have to do that," Walt said.

"It doesn't have nuts in it, does it?" Another gentleman came down the hallway, entering the living room. He looked like Walt, only slightly taller and missing the luscious locks of hair.

"Ladies, this is my brother, Gus. He just got in for Christmas. Gus, this is Celia and Wini. They live across the road."

Celia nodded a hello. Wini, on the other hand, perked up instantly and ran a hand through her hair. Once Wini began batting her eyes faster than someone in a sandstorm, Celia was more than happy to stand back and watch whatever happened next.

"So, what about the bread? Any nuts? Cause Walt will puff up and keel over if he's even in the same room as a nut."

Wini dove for the loaf, snatching it from Walt, who looked as stunned as if he just saw Santa himself shimmy down the chimney.

"Sorry, Walt. I had no idea." Wini clasped the loaf to her chest, hiding it from view with the stack of papers.

"Wouldn't be a holiday without someone trying to kill you off, huh, little brother?" Gus nudged Walt's shoulder with his own.

"Don't worry about it, Wini. I should probably get better about telling people I'm allergic."

"Um." Celia cleared her throat. "I also made you something."

She passed the wreath to Walt, fluffing the bow when he took hold of it.

"This morning I noticed you didn't have one on your door, and when I was in town earlier, I saw the fabric and just thought I'd whip one up."

"It's lovely, Celia. Thank you." He turned to Gus and pointed at the wreath. "Hey, I think that's us. Remember skating on Gordon's pond?"

"Phew, that was a lot of years ago." Gus rubbed a hand over his smooth head.

"Let's hang this up, shall we?" Walt smiled.

Walt and Gus started down the hall. Celia turned to follow, but Wini grabbed her sleeve.

"Isn't he dreamy?" Wini whispered.

"Walt?"

"No. Of course not. Gus." Wini sighed like a lovestruck teenager. "It's that bald head. I'm just a sucker for them."

"Probably because you can practically see your own reflection," Celia muttered.

"What dear?" Wini stood in the hall, preening, while Walt and Gus hung the wreath on the door.

"Too bad about that banana bread." Celia could have said anything she wanted, and Wini wouldn't have paid her any mind.

"Oh, yeah." Wini turned to her and gasped. "Celia, I just had the most exciting idea. You and Walt. Me and Gus. We'd be like sisters."

Celia's eyes went wide. She considered herself a tolerant and patient person in most instances, but the thought of Wini at her family gatherings was just too much.

"Gus doesn't even live here. You may never even see him again."

"A girl can dream, Ceels."

Walt and Gus returned, their cheeks rosy from their brief time in the cold. Win ilatched onto Gus's arm and drug him towards the couch, peppering him with questions about where he lived and what he liked to do. Celia almost felt bad for him, until she saw the smile on his face.

"The wreath is beautiful. And the personal details really make it something special." Walt placed a hand on her elbow, and they walked towards the kitchen. "Thank you. Can I interest you in some coffee? Or cocoa?"

"Honestly, a hot chocolate sounds delightful."

"Coming right up."

Celia leaned against the counter watching Walt move around his kitchen. Copper pots hung above his large gas range, glinting in the lights.

"So, I stopped in MistleTomes today and had a very strange conversation with Skye."Walt opened a large pantry, sifting through boxes until he pulled out a can of cocoa mix. "Something about front porch swings and lemonade. Then she told me to stay away from fancy restaurants. I couldn't make heads or tails out of what she was saying."

"Oh, you know Skye." Celia chuckled and waved it off, looking for anything else to talk about. "This is quite the kitchen, Walt. Do you do a lot of cooking?"

"Well, I was a chef for over forty years, so you could say I know how to whip up a few things."

"Walt! When you said you worked in restaurants, I assumed as a manager or something. I had no idea."

"Well, there's still plenty of stuff for us to learn about each other." He slid a cup of cocoa in front of her. "How about you come over for dinner once the holidays are over? I'll cook the entrée; you bake the dessert."

"I would really like that. I'm so glad you asked." Celia clasped the cup in both hands. "I can tell my daughter to call off the blitzkrieg."

"Huh?" Walt's brows pulled together in confusion.

"Well, this is rather embarrassing."

Celia filled him in on her conversation with Sarah that afternoon, nervously tucking her hair behind her ears as she spoke. She left out her most recent thoughts at taking her daughter up on it though.

"So, your daughter was going to ride over on a reindeer and rub peanut butter on my car door handles?" Walt grinned when Celia finished.

"I know. It sounds awful." Celia hung her head.

"I think it sounds like it would have been a heck of a story down the road." Walt leaned down on the counter so she could see his face. "You thought I was going out with Wini? Right after taking you out?"

"That's how it looked." Celia shrugged. "And Wini didn't exactly clear up the misunderstanding."

"Ah." Walt suddenly stood up. "Oh. Oh. Front porch swing." He pointed to himself. "Fancy restaurant?" He pointed out towards the living room.

Celia nodded.

"Lemonade?" Walt pointed at her.

Celia nodded again.

"Well," Walt walked over and opened the fridge. Inside was at least a half dozen bottles of lemonade, "that happens to be my favorite drink."

"And I happen to really enjoy porch swings." Celia could feel her chest expanding with joy. "That's the perfect combination if you ask me."

"I couldn't agree more." Walt grabbed both of their mugs and set them on the table. He pulled out a chair for Celia and sat down next to her.

"So, if she's fine dining," Walt tapped at his chin and whispered, "what does that make my brother?"

"In over his shiny head."

Nora

N ora pleaded with the sun to recede back below the horizon; maybe spin backward and reverse time for a few days. It couldn't be Christmas Eve. It just couldn't. She wasn't ready.

She turned from the window and felt her way through the near darkness, around the mattress on the floor where Elena and Julian slept. More than anything, she wanted to crawl under the blanket and snuggle with her babies and allow them one more day of hope and innocence. Belief in magic and Christmas. When they woke up tomorrow and found nothing under the tree and no food on the table, she'd have to figure out how to explain to them that she'd failed. Her heart cracked at the thought.

She shook off her dread for tomorrow and tugged on the maroon sweater her mother lent her when they'd moved back with little more than the clothes on their backs. Slowly, she turned the doorknob and eased out into the hall, quickly glancing back at her sleeping children.

Elena and Julian's lustrous curls were sprawled across their pillows, the only good thing their father ever gave them.

Nora closed the door and tiptoed down the short hallway. A crack of light under the kitchen door told her that her father was already awake. She grabbed her purse off the couch and joined him.

He stood at the scarred, laminate countertop running water through the same coffee grounds he'd used yesterday. And probably the day before that. Another crack to her heart.

Her father had worked hard to support her growing up; she shouldn't be back here expecting him to do it again. Especially after her parents were forced to move to Reverence Ridge after her mother's illness. But what choice did she have after getting laid off? For months, she'd tried to find a job, but when school let out for summer, she had no one to watch the kids. The bills piled up with no way to pay them. One day, they returned from the park to find the locks changed and their possessions thrown on the street. They carried what clothes they could to the train station and begged for enough money to buy tickets back to Reverence Ridge where her parents lived.

The air shuddered out of her as she went over those days for the thousandth time in her head. They'd walked up to her parents' house exhausted and starving. The kids thought staying with Gigi and Pop-Pop was amazing, but Nora thought they'd already overstayed their welcome.

"Morning, Dad," Nora muttered and patted him on the shoulder.

He grunted in response and walked to the table with his mug. Nora looked at the pot of barely brown water and cringed. She wanted to tell him she'd get more coffee in town today, but after so many days of broken promises, she just couldn't anymore.

Nora stared at the cracked vinyl beneath her feet, nothing like the nicely tiled kitchen she'd grown up in. Downsizing had been hard on both of her parents, but especially her father who'd put so much work into their previous home, thinking they'd retire and spend the rest of their days in that house. Cancer had a way of changing things.

Her father stood and set his mug in the sink next to her. Nora pulled her arms in tighter, making herself as small as possible, so she wouldn't be in the way.

"You comin'?" he asked from the door to the garage.

She followed him silently out to his '83 Ford pick-up. Her breath clouded in front of her, and she rubbed her arms against the cold. The garage door, which had broken months ago, was propped up with an old fencepost and offered no protection against the winter wind howling outside.

The door creaked open as she quickly slid in. Her breath was just as visible in the truck cab. Nora curled into herself, pulling the cardigan tightly around her. The truck rumbled to life, and they backed out onto the gravel road.

The foothills lay to the west of their house, rising slowly into the Smokies themselves. In the summer, their road was beautiful; flanked with lush fields and wildflowers. In the winter it was brutal. Wind rushed down the mountains and raced past their little house. That morning, she could hear it roaring over the sound of the engine. Pellets of snow swirled on the ground and through the air.

Sound was all around them, yet they sat silently as her father leaned over the steering wheel to see. She wanted to apologize. To tell him it would get better. That she'd finally found a job and was able to pitch in. She wanted to tell him so many things, but the silence was too heavy to lift with weak words.

The crunching of the tires on gravel changed to a whirring as they moved onto paved roads and entered city limits. Nora fingered a tear on the seat next to her, jagged and fraying. They slowed as her father turned onto the city square. It was early enough that some shops weren't open yet, and the tree in the center stood dark. Soon, the lights would come on and people would flood the stores, but right now it felt cold and empty. Her father pulled to a stop in front of the diner.

"Want a ride home?" he asked.

"No. I don't want you waiting if I'm able to find any work."

He simply nodded, and she slid out. She stood still in the road as he pulled away, heading towards the mechanic's shop he'd started working at when they'd moved here. Nora shivered as the wind easily blew straight through her thin cardigan. She hurried to the side of the diner, huddling against the building. At least it blocked the brunt of the wind.

This was the time of day she hated the most. It was too early to enter any of the shops to see about day jobs. Most mornings she brought one of her mother's novels. But she'd read them all multiple times, and it was too cold to have her fingers out and exposed anyway.

Stamping her feet, she turned and paced along the side of the building. Soon, she couldn't feel her legs, and her nose was starting to hurt. The last thing she needed was to get sick, or worse get frostbite. There was no way they could afford any more medical bills.

Her options were to stand outside and freeze, or possibly go stand in the diner's entryway, just for a few minutes until the other stores opened. If she huddled against the wall, maybe no one would even notice her there.

Nora crept around to the front of the building and was blasted with wind so cold it took her breath away. Her hair tangled around her face, blinding her as she pushed towards the entrance. A few more steps. That's what she kept telling her legs, which no longer had any feeling and felt like dead weight each time she lifted them.

Peering around the edge of the door, Nora made sure no one would see her. She quickly pulled it open just enough to squeeze through and eased it shut, which wasn't easy with the wind howling. Once inside, she sagged against the wall and closed her eyes. Her hands trembled when she raised them to brush the hair out of her face.

When was the last time she ate anything? She'd learned to ignore the ever-present gnawing in her stomach, but the looseness of her pants told her she'd been skipping meals a little too often. When the smell of coffee and bacon wafted under the door from the dining area, her knees threatened to buckle. She sagged against the wall and her chest tightened.

She could feel all the cracks of last few months. Guilt. Falilure. Despair. Hopelessness. They were all inside her, chipping away at her flimsy armor, threatening to burst through. She could feel them rising in her throat, pressing tears through her lashes, whispering in her ear. After several ragged breaths, she shoved them back down. It was getting harder every time, but she did not intend to have a nervous breakdown in the entryway of the diner.

"Hello, my dear," a soft voice startled her.

"Oh, good morning," Nora quickly swiped her hands under her eyes and turned toward the dining room. "I'm sorry, I'll be heading out in a second, I was just..." Nora quickly glanced around, desperate for a reason to be there. Her eyes fell on a bulletin board of posters, "...just looking at the job postings."

"*Mio cara*, you don't have to stand out in the cold. Come in. Come in." The old woman waved her inside.

The warmth soaked into her legs instantly, making them sting like pins and needles. Wrapping her arms tightly around her middle, she stopped just inside the door.

"Come on. Have a seat." The woman kept walking towards the stools at the counter. She hopped up and patted the one next to her.

Nora hesitated at the door. She didn't want to intrude, and she wasn't able to pay for anything.

"Um. I can't buy anything." Nora's voice wavered.

"I'm not expecting you to, *mio cara*." The woman swiveled and smiled. "Now, sit."

Nora walked slowly, glancing around. The only other time she'd been inside was when she'd asked for a job several months back. Most of her experience was in restaurants, so she thought this was her best shot. But they were already fully staffed and couldn't take on any more servers. Nora understood restaurants were a fickle business, but it had still stung.

She slid onto the stool and rested her hands on the counter. Her legs dangled above the floor, making her feel small.

"I remember you," the woman said. "I'm still sorry we couldn't give you a position here."

"It's ok. I understand."

"And I've seen you out there every morning. Still no job?"

Nora shook her head as her cheeks flamed in embarrassment. Did everyone see her? She'd tried to be as inconspicuous as possible.

"Don't be ashamed. That shows serious dedication. I've been impressed."

Nora finally turned to look at the woman. She looked like the world's most snuggly grandma decked out in restaurant garb.

"Remind me of your name, *mio cara*."

"Nora, ma'am." She hesitated briefly, but then asked, "What's *cara*?"

"My dear." The old woman's eyes looked distant. "One of the few words left over from my childhood in Italia."

"Was it beautiful there?"

"*Si.*" She grinned and focused back on Nora. "Breathtaking. And the food." She held her fingertips to her mouth and kissed them.

Nora smiled in return. Warmth had returned to her legs and nose, but she kept her fingers wrapped tightly in the sleeves of her cardigan.

"I am Marta. My husband, Nico, and I own this diner. And you are welcome in here any time." Marta leaned in to make sure Nora was listening. "You hear me? Any. Time."

"I don't want to intrude."

"Intrude?" Marta swept a hand around the room and laughed. "There's no one here. I'd welcome the company in the mornings."

"Um, ok. Thank you." Nora went back to staring at her hands on the counter.

"You, my dear, look like you have the weight of the world on your shoulders."

Nora didn't know what to say to that, so she said nothing at all. Marta slipped off her stool, patting Nora's leg. She shuffled back behind the counter and disappeared into the kitchen. She came back with two cups of coffee, one in a mug and one in a to-go cup, and something under her arm.

"I know you're a busy woman, but everyone needs a little extra pep in the mornings." Marta set the to-go cup in front of Nora.

"Oh, no, ma'am. That's ok. I couldn't possibly..." Nora sighed. "I can't pay for that."

"I'm not asking you to, am I?" Marta slid back into her stool. "It's a cup of coffee. Drink up."

They sat in silence, sipping at their drinks. Nora wanted more than anything to enjoy this simple gift, but all she could think about was the barely tinted water sitting in the pot at home that her dad endured every morning. Because of her. The coffee slid down her throat, hot and bitter.

"I know you haven't been here long," Marta said. "But there's something you should know about Reverence Ridge."

Marta waited until Nora looked over at her. The old woman had a thoughtful expression on her face.

"We're a community. We take care of our own." She slid the fabric she'd carried from the kitchen onto her lap. "You're one of us now. There are no strangers here. Just family. And family helps each other. Because you know what? I might need help tomorrow. And I know this town will be therefor me. So, if you'll let us, we'll be there for you, too."

She slid the fabric into Nora's lap. Nora lifted it up. A dark green button-down coat made of heavy fleece. She held it in front of her face until she was able to rein in her emotions.

"Miss Marta. This is too much." She lowered it and tried to slide it back to Marta's lap. "This is way too much."

"It's not. And you will keep it. I won't let you go backout in this horrid cold in just that sweater. You'll catch your death out there."

Nora continued to shake her head. Her parents raised her to work for what she got, not accept charity. Some could call it pride. She called it solid work ethic.

"Nora, consider it my Christmas gift to you."

"But I have nothing to offer in return."

"Promise you'll come see me in the mornings. Your company is all the gift I need."

"I can do that." Nora nodded and settled the coat into her lap.

"Now, you said you have worked in restaurants. Do you perhaps have any baking experience?"

"I washed dishes at a bakery in Savannah. That was my favorite job. Watching the decorators was like witnessing magic." Nora sighed at the memory. "But I never touched any of the equipment, unless it needed cleaning. I tried a few of the techniques at home with my kids too."

"Hm, well, that may be close enough." Marta pursed her lips to the side, thinking. "There's a poster in the entry way that may interest you, *mio cara*, but you'd need to hurry."

"Really?" Nora was off the stool and across the room before Marta finished.

Her eyes darted over the posters for guitar lessons, pet sitting, and the like. She finally spotted the one Marta mentioned.

Cookie Decorating Contest
Where: MistleTomes
When: Christmas Eve Day, 10 a.m.
1st place will receive prizes from local shops and a surprise offer

"I don't know what other businesses provided for prizes, but our contribution was a complete Christmas dinner, delivered tomorrow at noon." Marta had brought out Nora's coffee cup.

Nora sucked in a long breath. She'd watched pastry chefs make masterpieces in the bakery she worked at, and she'd often dreamed of doing the same. But dreaming and doing were nowhere near the same thing.

"I don't know, Miss Marta. I've never done anything like that."

"And you'll never know if you can unless you try." Marta shrugged. "It's the Christmas season, *mio cara*. Miracles do happen. Just believe."

"Just believe," Nora repeated and turned back to the poster.

"You need to register, so hurry over and make sure there's a spot for you."

Nora thought about it another moment before realizing she didn't have anything to lose. She slid an arm into the coat, relishing the weight of it, and chewed at her lip as she fastened the buttons up the front.

"Don't forget this." Marta held out the coffee. "You can do it. Don't doubt yourself for an instant, and no one else will either."

"Thank you so much, Miss Marta." Nora rubbed the sleeve of the coat with one hand and held her cup in the other. "I can't tell you how much this means to me."

"You'll pay it forward someday. That's how we work around here. If you're still job hunting after Christmas, you come talk to me. I wish I'd known sooner. We'll find you something."

"Thank you. Thank you." Nora shook her head in disbelief.

"You are welcome, *mio cara*. I look forward to our morning chats." Marta waved as Nora headed for the outside door. "Happy holidays, Nora."

"Same to you, Miss Marta." Nora waved and stepped outside.

The wind still blew, but she barely felt it through her new coat. A weak sun hung in a gray sky, but Nora guessed it had to be around eight o'clock and hurried down the sidewalk towards MistleTomes. A tiny seed of hope planted itself in her chest, strengthening her armor and filling a few of the cracks, but she kept it small. Letting hope grow too early could be just as damaging, sometimes more, than the constant strain of hopelessness. She'd had her dreams dashed one too many times to fall for that again.

The lights were on in the bookstore, and the doors unlocked, so Nora walked in. Two women sat at a covered table to the side of the entrance. A banner across the front had the word 'contest' written on it in blocky letters. They both looked up and smiled as Nora approached.

"Good morning. Are you here to register? Or have you already?"

"Um. I'd like to register, please." Nora cleared her voice, hoping to lose the tremble.

"Wonderful. Here are a few forms for you to fill out." They handed her a clipboard.

"Thanks," Nora said.

She walked a few steps away and went through the paperwork. One was basic personal information. Another was a questionnaire about her interests and any experience she had. After filling out so many job applications over the last few months, she had no trouble filling it all in.

She took the clipboard back to the table. One woman looked it over quickly, then glanced at her with a grin.

"Everything looks in order. I think we're going to have a couple great contestants today. We'll just need the $20 entrance fee and you're all set."

"The what?"

"Oh, the entrance fee. It's just to cover the cost of the materials for the contest."

"Um, I'm sorry. I don't have..." Nora's voice tapered off.

"Oh, we can take credit or debit." The woman held up a card reader. "Or a cash app if that's easier. We know nobody carries cash anymore.'

"I don't. Um. I don't have any of those," Nora mumbled and turned towards the door. "Sorry."

"We'll keep your papers on hand. Just in case you come up with the money. It's only $20," they hollered after her as she rushed out.

Hope was indeed a dangerous thing. Nora stopped just outside the door, clutching at her chest. Despair was like ice in her veins, forcing the cracks open even deeper. She gasped at the pain. She'd felt so close to giving her kids a Christmas they deserved. So close.

Breaking through her inner monologue of shame and doubt, she heard a long string of not very Christmas like words. Nora turned toward the street and saw a pair of legs sticking out of the trunk of an SUV surrounded with large boxes. She watched as the legs kicked and the rest of the person shimmied out of the trunk, dragging another large box.

Nora hesitated a moment. She recognized the woman as the owner of the bookstore. She'd talked to her about jobs as well. She watched another moment as Skye struggled to stack the boxes on the sidewalk without them toppling over. Nora never passed up an opportunity to offer her services in hopes that she'd be compensated. Even $10 would make a big difference today. Some fresh coffee and candy for tomorrow morning, maybe?

"Um, Miss." Nora approached Skye, wringing her hands. "Do you need some help?"

"Huh?" Skye puffed air out of the corner of her mouth to blow her purple bangs out of her eyes. "Oh. Yes, please. That would be wonderful."

"Ok." Nora placed her hands on the top box and tested the weight. "Where are these going?"

"Just inside the bookstore." Skye pointed with a foot as she lay half in the trunk and half out, pulling box after box.

Books were notoriously heavy, so Nora was surprised the boxes were as light as they were. She grabbed two and hurried inside. If she made quick work of this, maybe she could still find a few more odd jobs. A few bucks here and there added up. She set the boxes at the end of the checkout counter, making sure to keep her head down, hoping that the women at the registration table wouldn't notice her.

Skye was sitting on the edge of the trunk panting and raised a hand to wave when Nora rushed back out and grabbed more boxes, balancing three this time. Skye joined her on the next trip, struggling to carry two boxes while Nora breezed past her with three. By the fourth trip, Nora had worked up a sweat and her arms were beginning to burn. She picked her coffee up off the sidewalk and chugged the now cool contents before grabbing the last couple boxes.

Skye was leaning over the counter, breathing hard. Nora placed the last boxes next to the previous stack. The next part was what she hated most.

"Um, is there anything else I can do to help? Do you need these unboxed?" Nora stared at the floor, twisting a foot back and forth. "I'm looking for jobs today. To help out with Christmas."

"Oh, you're back." One of the registration women placed a hand on her shoulder. "Did you get a hold of the entry fee? I've still got your paperwork waiting here."

"That won't be necessary, Wanda. She won't require an entrance fee. Just write 'waived' on the paperwork for me, will you?" Skye said, still breathing heavily.

Nora's eyes shot up to Skye's face.

"That's too generous," she stammered.

"Are you kidding me? Look at me." Skye waved a hand around her face. "That would have taken me an hour, and you just blew past me and got it done in five minutes. That's the least I can do."

"Thank you," Nora said. Even though she didn't want it to return, the small seed of hope replanted itself next to her heart. Maybe, just maybe, Christmas miracles really did happen.

"Wonderful. While I'd love your help, these are all the supplies for the contest. So, it wouldn't be very fair for you to see everything ahead of everyone else."

"You're totally right." Nora took a step away from the boxes. "Is it ok if I just wait over here?"

"Of course. Grab a book and get comfy." Skye waved her off toward a sitting area in the back corner while the two registration ladies helped move the boxes towards the opposite side of the store.

The sitting area had several comfy looking armchairs. She knew she wouldn't be able to focus on reading, no matter how luxurious a new book sounded, so she just snatched up one at random and sunk into the chair.

This contest was definitely a long shot. She'd watched her dad work on an engine hundreds of times, but that didn't mean she'd jump under the hood of a car and expect to know what to do. How would cookie decorating be any different? Should she be wasting her time here? She could be out looking for legit, paying work.

The untouched book in her lap nearly fell to the floor as her leg bounced. She stared straight ahead, leg jumping at the speed of her racing thoughts. As much as she knew this was a gamble, she couldn't make herself stand up and leave.

Time ticked by, and the bookstore became more and more crowded as contestants arrived. She'd shed her new coat and old cardigan and was still sweating through her plain black t-shirt. Several other contestants wore their own aprons, some frilly, some brilliantly colored. Excited chatter filled the air around her, and she wiped moist palms against her jeans.

"Well, ladies and gentlemen, it's nine o'clock, which means it's officially contest time," Skye said from the other side of the store.

Nora moved with the crowd, inching towards the contest area, thinking that Skye sounded about as nervous as she felt. She held her coat tightly to her stomach, which was rumbling loudly. Whether from hunger or nerves, it wouldn't do to toss her cookies on the cookies. She prayed that it would settle once she got started.

"Hi. Yes, hello." Skye cleared her throat and shuffled from one foot to the other. "Thank you all for being here this morning. I'm excited to be hosting what I hope will be our annual decorating contest."

The crowd of about twenty people around her clapped before Skye continued.

"Would our five contestants step forward? I'm sure we're all excited to see who will be competing today."

Five contestants. That wasn't so bad. She'd been picturing a set-up like on Food Network with a dozen stations. Where had she thought that would fit in the small shop? She didn't know and was just glad her imagination had been wrong, as usual.

"Excuse me." Nora lowered her head and pushed towards the front of the crowd.

The lights suddenly felt very bright as Nora moved out of the group to join the other four ladies. She kept her eyes down, avoiding the stares of everyone before them. As long as she didn't have to say anything, she'd be fine. Imagining everyone in their underwear hadn't worked for her in high school speech class, and nothing had changed in the years since.

"I'll go ahead and introduce everyone quickly." Skye stepped out to point as Nora and the other four arranged themselves into a line. "We have Celia and her daughter, Sarah. A little family battle should be fun. Then we have Carol. I'm so glad you could be here. Next up is Nora. She's new to Reverence Ridge, so make sure to give her a big welcome. And finally, we have Kassie who's a junior at Ridge High."

Nora raised her head, but kept her eyes trained on Skye so she wouldn't see the crowd as they clapped again.

"Why don't you each go pick a station, and we'll quickly go over the rules."

The five ladies walked back to a series of folding tables set up with plastic tablecloths and a station at each end. The mother daughter duo took a table. The other two took the next one, leaving Nora to take the one at the back by herself. Relief rolled through her, loosening her shoulders and back, at the thought of being able to hide behind everyone else and not having to share her space.

"Ok. The rules." The tremor in Skye's voice had gone, and she was talking quickly now, obviously excited about starting. "We have a table of cookies here, already baked so you just have to focus on the decorations. There are about ten different shapes to choose from. On each table we have bowls of colored icing, piping bags, and spatulas. Embellishments, like sprinkles and candies, are on the table with the cookies. Take whatever you want. You have thirty minutes to decorate as many as you can. After that, the cookies will be judged by our local food experts."

Food experts? Nora wasn't sure who in Reverence Ridge would classify as an expert. She narrowed her eyes at the cookie table, but from this far back she couldn't make out any of the shapes.

"On your mark. Get set. Decorate!"

All five of them rushed to the table, but Nora hung back, not wanting to push in front of anyone. Each person took a plate full of cookies and snatched up the decorations, then rushed back to their tables. Nora stared at the cookies for quite a while, trying to make a plan. She grabbed up mostly gingerbread men, a sleigh, a Santa, and a simple rectangle. Then, she selected some sprinkles and candies she knew would go well with her idea.

Back at her table, she set the cookies out in a line. She knew Santa needed to be the centerpiece and decided to start on him. Her heart hammered up into her throat as she prepared to start. She needed this to work. Elena and Julian's Christmas depended on these thirty minutes.

Her hand trembled, dropping the Santa cookie to the table. It cracked down the center, a pain that Nora swore she felt. She rushed back to the cookie table and grabbed the last Santa available.

"Last one. Pull it together," Nora muttered to herself as she walked back to her table.

She closed her eyes and thought back to the bakery she'd worked in. Memories of the decorators came easily to mind, starting with filling piping bags. She folded the top down, inserted the tip, and scooped frosting of each color into the bags. Her first attempt ended up with dribbled yellow frosting across the table, but by the final color, she had a system.

Closing her eyes, she remembered them piping onto cookies. She knew how time consuming that was, waiting for each layer to dry before moving on to the next. Sometimes it would take them all day to get through decorating a single tray of cookies. Nora knew that wouldn't work here. She had thirty minutes, not thirty hours.

Could she choose a main color and dip them to save time? It couldn't hurt to try, as long as it wasn't on the last Santa.

She picked up a gingerbread man and pulled the bowl of brown icing in front of her. She slowly dipped the top of the cookie, wiping the extra drips off on the side of the bowl as she pulled it up. She quickly flipped it over and remembered another technique from the bakery. Icing would often get air bubbles in it that would ruin the final finish. Nora gently tapped the cookie on the table to bring any bubbles to the surface and ran a toothpick through to smooth them out.

The first one didn't look too bad, she decided, so she went ahead and dipped the rest. She prayed this base coat would have time to dry before she started the actual decorating. The ladies at the table in front of her were chatting, but Nora tried to block out their voices. If she didn't give this her full attention, she'd never forgive herself.

The minutes ticked by as she added piping details. She knew to twist the bag at the top, so the icing didn't squeeze out all over her hand. Even knowing this, she still did it multiple times. The decorators had made their squeeze-twist method look so easy, but it took all of Nora's concentration. Once the icing was applied, she strategically added sprinkles and candies.

Everyone else melted away as she focused on bringing her vision to life. Once she was in the groove, it was easy to block out the talking around her. Even the people walking around to take peeks didn't bother her like they did everyone else. Just as she was brushing a little watered down red coloring on her Santa's cheeks, Skye called out the end of the contest.

"Times up, ladies. Piping bags down." Skye raised her hands in the air like on the cooking shows. "Phew. That was intense."

Nora looked down at what she'd created. Decorating was more physically demanding than she'd imagined. She massaged her tingling forearms and tried to stretch out the kink in her back.

"We'll move on to judging as soon as everyone gets their cookies onto a tray and leaves their stations."

Nora gently lifted the cookies up with her fingertips so she wouldn't smudge the icing. She placed her smiling Santa in the bottom corner of the tray. He stood next to his sleigh, which she'd dotted with snowflake sprinkles. In front of that, she placed nine gingerbread men cookies that she'd flipped upside down to create reindeer. Their legs became antlers, their arms ears, and the head was now an adorable little muzzle. Eight had brown sixlet noses. Rudolph had a cinnamon candy nose. Above them all, she placed the rectangle that she'd decorated with a blue background and a golden shooting star.

"I wish, I wish with all my might," she whispered as she placed the star on the tray, "grant the wish I wish tonight."

Wishing on a star cookie before lunchtime might not have as much power as wishing on the first star of the night, but she'd take whatever luck she could get. Nora left her tray at the end of her table and walked toward the crowd.

On the station in front of her, she saw some nice-looking wreath cookies, and atthe other end, a mix of every shape possible. The mother and daughter duo looked like they had a sprinkle war. Their cookies probably weighed about a pound each with the amount of icing and decorations. The daughter was currently pulling sprinkles out of her mother's hair.

"I believe both of our local food experts have just arrived, so they won't know who goes with which cookies. Let's bring them out here." Skye waved them forward. "We have Mindy from Cup of Cheer and Marta from Wonderful Thyme."

The crowd, including Nora this time, applauded. So that's why Marta had suggested this? She was a judge. Since it was blind judging, Nora knew that wouldn't give her any advantage, and she didn't want it to. If she was going to win, it needed to be earned. She tried to contain it, but the hope in her chest grew bigger.

Skye, Marta, and Mindy moved back through the decorating tables, pointing at cookies and talking in hushed voices. When they came to her tray, Nora covered her eyes. She peeked through her fingers a few times but could barely stand to watch.

If she didn't win this, she'd wasted half a day of job hunting on cookies. An image of Elena and Julian waking up to an empty house in the morning tore at her heart. Her babies deserved a Christmas. They knew all the holiday stories. They'd been extra good, especially considering their circumstances. The last six months had been so stressful, but you wouldn't know it looking at them. She needed this win for them.

But she also needed this win for herself. The guilt and shame grew more and more each day that she didn't provide for her family. A win would hush those voices inside that she wasn't good enough. So, yes. She needed this. Badly.

Skye walked toward the group again, a smile on her face. Marta and Mindy flanked her, also smiling. Nora dropped her hand to her chest, wrapping her fingers in the neckband of her t-shirt.

"A winner has been selected. There are a lot of beautiful creations up here, so this was tough. But one person stood ahead of the rest."

Blood pumped in Nora's ears as her eyes narrowed in on Skye. Pleading with the star for luck, she prayed over and over.

"Our first-place winner will receive gift cards to Wizzle's, Cup of Cheer, Tin Soldier, and here, MistleTomes. Marta at Wonderful Thyme has been generous enough to offer a full Christmas meal, catered tomorrow."

That was so much more than she'd expected. Those gift cards could be life-changing for her. She squeezed her eyes shut.

"And the winner, who made one heck of a tray of cookies, is..." Skye paused, "Nora."

Nora gasped, and her eyes flew open. Did she hear right? Was that her name? She'd really done it? She felt hands on her elbow pushing her forward. Her ears finally registered the applause around her, and she took another step.

Marta walked over to meet her and pulled her into a hug.

"I knew you could do it, *mio cara*." She gave her a final squeeze and urged her toward Skye.

"Congratulations, Nora," Skye said. "Your cookies are just beautiful. And, as Marta tells me, you did this with no actual decorating experience?"

"No, ma'am."

"You're just a natural." Mindy reached around and patted her on the shoulder. "Well done. I'd sell those cookies in my shop any day of the year."

"Really? Thank you," Nora stammered. She felt like she was swimming through molasses, just trying to keep up.

"Want to come back to my office and I'll get your prizes?" Skye smiled and turned toward the back corner of the store. Mindy moved in behind them to address the crowd.

Nora barely felt her feet touch the floor as they walked through a door. The room didn't register at first. Not until Skye pulled a stool up to a stainless steel, industrial-sized island. Nora looked around at a spotless kitchen.

"This is your office?" she asked.

"Not quite, but I wanted to bring you in here." Skye looked around fondly and rubbed her hand over the countertop. "I don't know if you remember on the flyer, it said there'd be a surprise offer for the 1st place winner?"

"Um." Nora tried to remember anything about the flyer, but her mind was all aflutter. "No, I don't. Sorry."

"Well, it did." Skye laughed.

"So, there's more than just the gift cards?" Nora leaned against the counter.

"I've always wanted to offer food here. I started talking to Mindy about doing some kind of cooperative thing between the bookstore and coffeeshop, but we just couldn't figure out how it would work with only one kitchen. So, I had this one put in."

"Ok?" Nora didn't see where this was headed.

"I was really impressed with you today. You're a hard worker, and you were totally cool under pressure out there."

"I was? I felt like a nervous wreck."

"Could have fooled me." Skye shrugged.

The door flew open, and Mindy and Marta walked in.

"Did you ask her yet?" Mindy tapped her fingertips together in excitement.

"I'm just getting to it." Skye shushed her.

"Ask me what?" Nora's voice cracked. She wasn't sure what was going on.

"You're obviously talented. And you have restaurant experience, so you're pretty perfect." Skye took a deep breath. "Nora, would you like to run my kitchen?"

"Are you... Are you offering me a job?" Nora whispered.

"Yes, silly." Mindy clapped in excitement.

Nora's knees buckled as a sob erupted from inside her. Marta was at her side, pulling her onto a stool. Tears poured down her cheeks, and great sobs shook her. All the negative feelings drained from her body, pushed out by that little seed of hope. The other three women surrounded her, patting her back and comforting her.

"You have... no idea... what this means." Nora sobbed.

"Hopefully that you accept the job?" Skye asked.

"Yes, yes. Of course." Nora's sobs turned to laughter, which tapered off into hiccups.

"Thank God," Mindy sighed.

Skye pulled sandwich fixings out of the fridge, and they talked for about an hour over lunch. They hadn't worked out all the fine details about the job yet. She would mainly work at MistleTomes but would collaborate with the coffeeshop. They made a plan for her to return in several days to start figuring out the specifics and get the kitchen up and running.

"Now that's settled, how about you take your winnings and go get some gifts for that family of yours?" Skye handed her an envelope full of gift certificates.

"Yes. I need to do that before everyone closes." Nora grabbed her coat off the counter, ready to bolt out the door. "Thank you all. This is the best gift I could have possibly hoped for this year."

"I'm looking forward to working with you, Nora." Skye waved as she walked out.

Marta joined her on the way out of the store. Nora couldn't wipe the smile off her face. Once they were outside, she turned to Marta.

"Was that you? Did you make that happen?" Nora asked.

"Of course not. I just told Skye about your dedication after we'd decided you were the winner. The rest was all on them."

"Ok." Nora wasn't sure she believed her. "Thank you."

"You're a Ridger now, *mio cara*."

"I guess I am. See you tomorrow."

Nora waved goodbye and raced across the square to Wizzle's Wonders. She picked out several gifts for each of the kids and was even able to get them gift wrapped. Next, she walked to Tin Soldier to buy ingredients for a Christmas worthy breakfast, coffee included. Lastly, she stopped back at MistleTomes to pick out several new books for her mom.

By the time her father got off work, she was sitting on the tailgate surrounded with bags, swinging her legs like she did when she was a little girl.

"What's all this?" her father's weary voice weighed on her.

"It's Christmas." She hopped down and wrapped him in a hug. "I got a job today, Dad. A full-time, permanent job."

"You did?" He perked up.

"Yep. No more watered-down coffee for you."

"A Christmas miracle," he whispered.

"They do exist."

They stopped by Cup of Cheer to get bowls of soup, some crusty rolls, and pastries for dinner. When her father clicked on the truck radio, sipping at a large cup of dark roast, Nora knew they'd be ok.

She leaned her head on the window, listening to a church choir and watching the large pines whisk by. The mountains stood dark against the evening sky. The truck left the paved roads of Reverence Ridge. As they bounced down their gravel lane, she could feel the cracks in her armor healing. They'd never disappear, scars never did, but the pain was gone.

Nora looked up just in time to see a golden light streak across the sky. In her heart, she knew that was her little seed of hope, off to harass, torment, and save someone else.

"Thank you," she whispered against the glass. "Merry Christmas."

If you enjoyed *Christmas in Reverence Ridge*, check our the latest anthology from Kaleidoscope Author Co-op:

Warmth In Winter

Skye, the owner of MistleTomes, goes on a hot cocoa fueled quest, and maybe, just maybe, stumbles into her knight in shining armor along the way.

Check out "A Long Dark Night" by Elaina Kellogg in this exclusive sneak peek.

A Long Dark Night

Winter Solstice was the darkest day of the year, and even at the ungodly early hour of 5 a.m., that deep darkness only filled Skye with a sense of wonder. While some people might be afraid of the night, Skye always relished it. The peace. The quiet. Those hours were when her heart sang, and her mind pondered all sorts of possibilities.

"Too bad civilization was designed by those darn early birds," Skye muttered to herself as she turned her car to roll slowly down the empty street. "Night owls need to revolt."

Then she shuddered at the thought of society becoming nocturnal, and all those people encroaching into her beautiful hours of solitude.

"Nope. Never mind, Universe. Forget I said anything." Shivers ran down her spine again. "That sounds horrible."

There was some truth to that saying about there being three kinds of people. Early birds, night owls, and some sort of permanently exhausted pigeon. Skye fell into the third category, forced into the early hours to run her business, but still enjoying the late hours of night in her personal time. It left her with bags under her eyes and a tiredness that had seeped into her bones. Especially this time of year.

Christmas in the town of Reverence Ridge was truly something to behold. Even in the dark, Skye smiled at the wreaths gracing every door and lamp post. The garlands laid along fences and flower beds. The poinsettias on porches. The people of Reverence Ridge did a lot of things well, but they excelled at Christmas.

Skye pulled into her usual spot outside her shop, MistleTomes, her mind full of all the things she needed to complete before the store opened. With a final stretch and yawn, she slid out into the chill of early morning. She lifted her long, flowy skirt, stepped over the snow heaped at the curb, and dodged the small patches of ice glistening in the faint hint of morning light. Salt crunched under her Converse sneakers as she picked her way across the sidewalk toward the front door.

Skye slid her key into the lock and hurried inside. Her shoulders instantly relaxed as warmth seeped in through her sweater. Without flipping any of the light switches, she made her way past bookshelves and tables of trinkets, to the plastic hanging along the back wall.

Skye glanced around, realizing it was silly to be so secretive inside an empty bookstore, and slid behind the large tarp. She ran her hand along the wall until she felt the cool metal of the doorknob. Then she paused.

A faint strip of light shone under the door, and that could mean only one thing.

"Taylor Callaway." Skye smiled as she stepped into the room. "Don't you ever sleep?"

"Not between Thanksgiving and New Year. Here, hold this for me, would ya?"

Skye rushed over to take a drill from Taylor as he worked on a light fixture over his head. Skye took in his tousled brown hair, getting a little longer than he usually kept it, and the strong lines of his back. His family's company name, Callaway Contracting, was emblazoned across his long-sleeved shirt.

"So, uh, whatcha doin' up there?" She set the drill onto the stainless-steel island in the center of the room and turned back to hold the ladder, something her grandpa had told her was always best for safety.

"Your final light fixtures came in yesterday, so I figured I'd come on over and get them hung up." He stopped twisting wires and looked down at her, leaning on the top step. "I didn't think you were going to be in today. Thought maybe I could surprise you. Shoulda known better. Can't keep you away from this place, even when you take the day off, huh?"

"I only had a few, itsy, bitsy things," she held up her fingers, squinting as she moved them closer together, "to do this morning."

"Itsy, bitsy, huh?" Taylor shook his head and flashed her a grin. "Like move the entire romance section in front of the fireplace? Oh! Or organizing the store by the Dewey decimal system?"

"The Dewey decimal system is for libraries and would be totally inefficient for a bookstore." She tilted her head, pondering. "But I do like the idea about the romance section being by the fireplace. We could bring the heat in more ways than one, huh? Huh?"

She waggled her eyebrows as steamy marketing puns ran through her mind. Taylor groaned as he climbed down the ladder.

"That was a joke, Skye." His warm eyes found hers, and he looked at her in mock sternness. "Go enjoy your day off. I assume you took it for a reason."

"It's the Winter Solstice." Skye shrugged and handed Taylor the drill.

Taylor nodded as he tossed his tools into his massive toolbox. Skye's fingers flexed, itching to get into those tools to organize them, so she walked around to the other side of the island. Leaning onto her elbows, she watched Taylor toss more tools inside, a wire stripper on top of a screwdriver, some wire nuts in with regular screws.

"How do you even function?"

"Pretty decently, I'd like to think." Taylor gave her his sauciest lopsided grin and then, without breaking eye contact, reached into the toolbox and swirled his hand around, messing up the contents even more.

"If I could have ten minutes with that-"

"Nope. We talked about this. Keep your neat, tidy hands off my tools."

"How about five minutes?"

"Skye." Taylor's voice was a combination of fake sternness edged with humor.

"Ugh, fine. Live in your squalor, heathen."

"Thank you." He nodded his head at her in acceptance. "Now, what do you think?"

Taylor walked over to the wall and unplugged his shop lamp throwing the room into complete darkness. Then, Skye heard the click of one switch, then another. First, the lights around the exterior of the room came on, then the hanging lights above the island. Stainless steel gleamed all around them.

"I think that's perfect." Skye stepped back to take in the entire commercial kitchen. "These give extra light here for more detailed work, while still keeping the rest of the room well-lit."

"It was a great idea." Taylor came to stand next to her in the corner, taking in everything they'd been working on over the past couple of months. "Whoever works in here is going to be one lucky chef."

Skye did a little shimmy, dancing on the balls of her feet. The thought of unveiling the new kitchen to the people of Reverence Ridge made her giddy. Since she was a young girl, she'd dreamed of owning a bookstore with a little café, so people could sip warm beverages as they lounged to read the latest bestseller, or nibble on a pastry as their kids listened to story time. And this kitchen was finally going to make those dreams come true.

"I can't thank you enough for all this." She bumped her shoulder into his and smiled up at him. "Free cookies for life."

"You seriously don't have to do that." Taylor shook his head, his chestnut hair falling onto his forehead.

Skye resisted the urge to brush it back, barely. Instead, she tucked a long purple strand of her own curls behind her ears. Between finally fully realizing her dreams, and also getting to work so closely with Taylor Callaway, the past few months had been a jumble of nerves and excitement.

"You're officially done," Skye said softly, her mood shifting instantly.

"Yep. And then you get a break from me. For a whole three days." Taylor rocked back on his booted heels.

"And what happens in three days?" Skye turned to him, arching a brow and wondering what he was getting at.

"You have your huge reveal at the cookie decorating contest, finally announce to the town you're opening your cafe so I can stop keeping the secret, and I start coming in for a little eat and read every day for lunch. You and your staff are going to be thoroughly sick of me."

"I don't think that would be possible." As quickly as her mood had dipped, it rose again. This wasn't the end, just a change.

Taylor grabbed his toolbox and carried it out to his truck as Skye took a final glance around the kitchen. Everything was in place. Every drawer was stocked with utensils. She'd used the ovens for the first time a few days ago, making lunch for Taylor's entire crew after they put up the massive tree in the town square to decorate for Christmas. Everything worked at peak performance, especially Taylor. He'd worked a lot of long hours in the evenings after the bookshop was closed to keep this secret for her.

"Definitely cookies for life," she mumbled as he walked back in.

"Let me grab this ladder, then I'll be out of your hair so you can get your work done and go enjoy your Winter Salsa."

"Winter Salsa?" Skye laughed. "You mean Winter Solstice?"

"Isn't that the same thing?" Taylor's eyes twinkled as he folded up his ladder and lowered it to the floor.

"Not even close. Winter Salsa does sound delicious though. What would that even have in it?"

"Cranberries, orange slices, mint. Served on cinnamon chips."

"Did you... did you just come up with the most delicious-sounding recipe off the top of your head?"

"Maybe I did. I expect full credit if that goes on the menu."

"Callaway's Christmas Salsa." Skye waved a hand in front of her, envisioning the name on the menu.

"Taylor's Tasty Treat." He leaned in and waved his hand in front of her.

"You are a tasty treat."

Skye sucked in a breath the instant the words came out of her mouth. Her mom always told her the lack of a filter would get her in trouble someday.

"Back at ya, cookie boss."

Taylor snatched up his ladder and was through the door with a smirk before Skye could even register what had happened.

"Did... did Taylor Callaway just flirt with me?" Skye spun around and asked the empty room.

For the rest of Skye's story, check out
Warmth in Winter
Releasing December of 2024.

ALSO BY
KALEIDOSCOPE
AUTHOR CO-OP

SONGS of SEAS and STARS

Madeline Dau   R.A. Krueger
Chelsea M. Brown   Katharine Bost

Maureen Marquette · Katharine Bost
Madeline Dau · Elaina Kellogg

Light AND Longing

Simply Sweet

T he Darlin' Diner was exactly as Lexi remembered it from the only time she'd been there almost twenty years ago. The late summer sun glinted off the aluminum siding, momentarily blinding her as she staggered out of the car. She felt all thirteen-hundred miles she'd driven over the past two days as she stretched and rolled her shoulders.

The Mississippi air was heavy with humidity and the scent of plants and earth. No other place she'd been smelled like this, smelled so green. Lexi pulled in a deep breath and smoothed her skirt before heading towards the entrance. The neon red and blue 'open' sign flashed in the front window as she pulled open the door.

The temperature change between the steamy heat outside and the frigid air-conditioned inside was shocking. Lexi debated turning back to grab a sweater, but excitement pushed her forward.

She slid into the first booth on the right side, just like she'd done as a little girl. The cherry red vinyl seat had faded slightly from years of sun pouring through the windows. Her fingers caressed the tear down the center of the bench, a smile tugging at her lips.

"Can I help you?"

Lexi looked up at the waitress in her polka dot uniform and apron, its cut very similar to her own vintage-inspired dress.

"Yes, Rosita," Lexi read her nametag, "I'd like a grilled cheese please."

"Just a grilled cheese?"

"Do you still do Free Fry-day?" Lexi said in a low voice, looking around, not wanting to share the secret, but the diner was practically empty since she'd arrived in those odd hours between breakfast and lunch.

"Free Fry-day?" The waitress, Rosita, looked confused. "Um. No."

"Ok. Well, I'll get fries too." Lexi was disappointed for a second before perking up again. "Oh, and a pop. Sprite, please."

"Pop? I knew I hadn't seen you before, but now I really know you aren't from around here."

"Nope. But I will be soon." Lexi wiggled her shoulders in excitement. "I'm moving here. Today actually."

"Well, congratulations. And welcome to Fauna."

Rosita turned to go, scribbling the order in her small notepad, but turned back when Lexi cleared her throat.

"Um," Lexi held up a finger. "I know this is a long shot, but does a Silvia still work here?"

"Silvia, yeah." Rosita's eyes narrowed. "Why?"

"Oh, I was just curious. She was my waitress last time I was here."

"Sheesh. When was the last time you were here? Mama hasn't been a waitress since I was a kid."

"Silvia is your mom?" Lexi asked.

"Yeah. She's in the back office." Rosita nodded her head towards the swinging door set back behind the counter. "I'll let her know you're here..."

"Lexi." She reached out and shook Rosita's hand a little more vigorously than needed. "Lexi Caehill."

"Right. I'll let her know you're here, Lexi." She gave a small smile before disappearing behind the swinging door.

Lexi had waited so long for this day; she couldn't believe it was finally here. Nervous energy poured out of her. She crossed her ankles and uncrossed them, then strummed her fingers on the spotted tabletop. When her toes began tapping along with the Elvis song crooning from the Jukebox in the corner, she started to even annoy herself. She knit her fingers together and shoved them in her lap, pressing down on her legs as if that would keep her toes rooted to the floor.

She stared down at her hands clenched on top of her skirt and remembered the hours her mother made her sit like this as a child. It wasn't ladylike to fidget she'd say as a wooden spoon snacked down over Lexi's knuckles. As if being ladylike was the height of their concerns. Eventually, she'd started sitting with her hands clasped in her lap all the time to avoid her mother's attention.

Lexi quickly pulled them apart, hating that, even at the age of twenty-eight, and from halfway across the country, she still feared her mother's judgments and wanted her approval.

"It's always a good idea to start a meal with prayer," said a voice over Lexi's shoulder. "That is what you're doing, isn't it?"

Lexi looked up and smiled. Even after so many years, she recognized the woman who'd offered her so much kindness as a child.

"I wish, Miss Silvia."

The older woman set her sandwich and a heaping plate of French fries on the table and slid into the booth across from Lexi. Her dark wavy hair had streaks of grey now, but her face hadn't been changed by time. Only the crinkles at the corners of her eyes hinted at the happy years she'd lived.

"I'm not sure if you remember me, but..." Lexi choked off the sentence, not sure what to say now that the moment had arrived.

"Of course, I remember you. As soon as Rosita told me there was a girl..." Silvia tilted her head and really looked at Lexi "... young woman asking about Free Fry-day I knew it must be you or your sister."

"I can't believe you remember that after all these years." Lexi's chest felt tight.

"How could I forget? Jeb Thompson heard me tell your mom about Free Fry-days and I've had to feed him free french fries every week for the last sixteen or seventeen years."

"Wait, so Free Fry-days wasn't really a thing?"

"Eh," Silvia waved a hand at her, "you and your sister were so scrawny. And those parents of yours not wanting to get you proper food. No one leaves my diner hungry."

As Lexi had grown older, she'd often wondered if Free Fry-day was something Silvia had made up to feed two hungry kids and not insult their prideful parents. It made her even more grateful to her.

"I can't even begin to tell you how much your kindness meant to me. I've wanted to come back so many times to thank you."

"Oh, niña," Silvia stopped and placed her hand over Lexi's, "it was just a couple plates of fries. Did it really mean that much to you?"

Lexi felt tears well in the corner of her eyes. She wanted to tell Silvia that it was so much more than just plates of fries. That it was the gesture. The pure, simple kindness, that left its mark on her. It was the fact that she'd noticed her. But the words just wouldn't come.

This wasn't going at all how she planned. She wanted to show Silvia how far she'd come from those days of being dragged from one state to another, hopping from one couch to the next. She did not want to revert into the small, scared child she'd been the last time she sat here in this booth. But sometimes going back to places of your childhood brought that part of yourself to the surface and Lexi couldn't fight the tears that spilled down her cheeks. She grasped Silvia's hand tightly, savoring the warmth of the touch.

"Child," Silvia leaned in and whispered, as if she'd read Lexi's mind, "you aren't that little girl anymore. Let it go and be happy."

"You're right." Lexi sniffled and wiped the tears away, smudging her eyeliner in the process. "I pictured this going so differently."

"Things happen as they are meant to." Silvia squeezed Lexi's hand before letting go and leaning back. "Maybe those tears have been waiting for just the right moment to leave you, which means you have been carrying them for a long time. Uncried tears are a heavy, heavy burden."

Lexi straightened in her seat, feeling the weight of each of those tears leaving her. She smiled at Silvia and popped a fry into her mouth.

"Mmm. You seriously make the best french fries I've ever had. And trust me, I've eaten a lot of them." Lexi stopped to squirt ketchup onto her plate. "French fries are not something they teach in culinary school, which is a real shame. Because, seriously, what beats a delicious plate of fries? Nothing. That's what."

"Culinary school? Is that what you've done with yourself?"

"Yes, ma'am." Lexi beamed. "But not for anything like french fries. I'm a pastry chef."

"I'm proud of you, niña. That is a big accomplishment. And your sister? Did she better herself as you have?"

"Uh, not really." Lexi set down her perfectly grilled cheese sandwich. "She hops from one job to another. One couch to another with my folks."

"Well, then what you have achieved is even more of an accomplishment. It is not easy to rise above what people expect of you."

The door jingled behind them, and Lexi watched as Silvia's face lit up. She heard several heavy steps beside her before the newcomer bent over to hug Silvia. Lexi's swallowed hard as the most perfect man's backside she'd ever seen graced her vision.

Lexi was liking Fauna, Mississippi more and more every second.

Check out early release chapters on Kindle Vella now!
Paperback and eBook releasing spring of 2025.

About the Author

ELAINA KELLOGG

Elaina Kellogg loves love. As a child, she fell in love with anything fluffy. In college, she fell in love with her husband. When her son was born, she fell head over heels in love. Now, she writes sweet, cozy stories of made-up people falling in love. She also loves witty banter. And pie. Who doesn't love pie? She's also one of those people who starts listening to Christmas music in September. Because it makes her feel lovely.

Feel free to follow her for badly filmed and sporadically posted content.

TikTok: @elaina_kellogg_author
BlueSky: @elainakellogg
Facebook: @elainakelloggwrites

www.ingramcontent.com/pod-product-compliance
Lightning Source LLC
Chambersburg PA
CBHW071854220626
47052CB00002B/114